T0165595

**Torrie watched intently as Masterson
mixed a pair of martinis for them
and brought the drinks to the couch.**

As the cool martini slid down her throat, she kept
her eyes locked on Masterson. She put down her
glass and used her now-free hand to trace a finger
along his jawline. Continuing down to his shoulder
and his arm, she took his glass out of his hand and
put it down on the coffee table. Still looking directly
into his eyes, she pushed the tiny button on her ring
that sent a stream of clear liquid into his glass. At the
same time, she distracted him with a kiss.

Masterson kissed back hungrily. His hands started
exploring her body, quickly going places where they
weren't exactly welcome. Torrie was silently thankful
for his desperate aggression. It made it easier to push
him away. With a smile, she took her glass and lifted it
to her lips as if she was only delaying the inevitable.
Masterson mirrored her move by taking his own glass.

After they both put their glasses back down, Torrie
responded to his earlier moves, giving him a look that
said, "You may proceed." And he did just that. He proceeded to pass out on the couch, thanks to the sedative
in his drink.

BIG APPLE TAKEDOWN

a novel by
Rudy Josephs

World Wrestling
Entertainment®

POCKET BOOKS

NEW YORK LONDON TORONTO SYDNEY

The sale of this book without its cover is unauthorized. If you purchased this book without a cover, you should be aware that it was reported to the publisher as "unsold and destroyed." Neither the author nor the publisher has received payment for the sale of this "stripped book."

POCKET BOOKS, a division of Simon & Schuster, Inc.
1230 Avenue of the Americas, New York, NY 10020

This book is a work of fiction. Names, characters, places and incidents are products of the author's imagination or are used fictitiously. Any resemblance to actual events or locales or persons, living or dead, is entirely coincidental.

Copyright © 2006 by World Wrestling Entertainment, Inc. All Rights Reserved.

World Wrestling Entertainment, the names of all World Wrestling Entertainment televised and live programming, talent names, images, likenesses, slogans and wrestling moves, and all World Wrestling Entertainment logos and trademarks are the exclusive property of World Wrestling Entertainment, Inc. Nothing in this book may be reproduced in any manner without the express written consent of World Wrestling Entertainment, Inc.

This book is a publication of Pocket Books, a division of Simon & Schuster, Inc., under exclusive license from World Wrestling Entertainment, Inc.

All rights reserved, including the right to reproduce this book or portions thereof in any form whatsoever. For information address Pocket Books, 1230 Avenue of the Americas, New York, NY 10020

ISBN 978-1-4516-3180-7

This Pocket Books paperback edition July 2006

10   9   8   7   6   5   4   3   2   1

POCKET and colophon are registered trademarks of Simon & Schuster, Inc.

Visit us on the World Wide Web
http://www.simonsays.com
http://www.wwe.com

Manufactured in the United States of America

For information regarding special discounts for bulk purchases, please contact Simon & Schuster Special Sales at 1-800-456-6798 or business@simonandschuster.com.

BIG APPLE TAKEDOWN

Prologue

PEPSI CENTER
ALBANY, NEW YORK

One!
Two!
Three!

From his backstage office, Vincent K. McMahon, chairman of World Wrestling Entertainment, thought the arena eruption sounded like two jet planes roaring overhead a stadium at the end of "The Star-Spangled Banner." There were five or so seconds where he couldn't hear anything except for the noise. Only twenty thousand angry fans make a sound that loud. Just about every one of those fans hated Triple H. Watching him regain the WWE Championship was torture for them, but hearing the passion in their reaction let Vince know that tonight's show was a winner. The fans were moved by what had unfolded in front of them.

Vince kept his eye on the TV monitor for another few minutes as he packed his briefcase. Once he saw Triple H hop off the ring apron, Vince hustled out of the room.

Backstage at the Pepsi Center looked the same as it did at the end of just about every WWE show. A mixture of Superstars, wives, girlfriends, office workers, stage crew, stadium personnel, and assorted random people who managed to get in were all standing around with smiles on their faces. It wasn't just Vince. They all knew the show had been a success.

Vince loved this time of the night. Everyone was laughing, having a beer, or hanging with their friends. That meant the show had gone off without a hitch. His Superstars had a blast performing and the fans were ecstatic. More importantly, though, he liked this time of night because it let him look ahead.

Okay, tonight went great, time to start working on tomorrow.

Anyone who knew Vince McMahon knew that no

matter what else was going on around him, regardless of what type of meeting he was in or new T-shirt design he was being presented, there was always one question at the front of his mind: *What's next?*

As he made his way around backstage, most everyone looked over at him to say something.

Great show tonight, boss.

The Pay-Per-View card is really coming together.

We blew 'em away tonight, Mister McMahon!

Usually Vince would stop, say hello, and thank everyone for the good show. He'd ask them what *they* thought about it, because he valued every opinion. Most of them he already knew, but every now and then someone would say something that would spark an idea for the future. Tonight he didn't have time for any of that. He should have been halfway down the New York State Thruway by now, but there was no chance of him leaving a show early, let alone *this* show. He was just about set to head out to the car, but needed to see his champion quickly before he left.

"Mister McMahon! Mister McMahon!" someone shouted from behind. Vince knew the voice without having to turn around. It was a voice he'd heard in the backstage of arenas for over three decades.

"Yes, Howard?"

"Sorry to bother you, Mister McMahon," said

Howard Finkel, known to generations of WWE fans as "The Fink." "But I was just talking to Tony, and he said you guys really ought to get on your way as soon as you can with this weather. And I told him that maybe you guys should just stay the night."

"Thanks, Howard," Vince said as he pushed past the guy. "I'll take that under advisement."

True to his word, Vince thought about pushing back his trip for the briefest moment, then shoved the idea right out of his mind. Of course he would have preferred to stay in Albany for the night. Any idiot would. Aside from not having to deal with the snow, it would give him some time to gather Triple H and Stone Cold Steve Austin to discuss their match at Madison Square Garden. However, his meeting with the guys at the network couldn't wait. If he didn't show, they might take it upon themselves to move forward with their promotional plans without his signoff. And that was not going to happen.

Vince headed toward the catering room, where he knew Triple H would be chowing down on his regular postmatch meal. He could only imagine what Tony, his driver, was thinking right now. Even if the weather predictions from earlier were only partially correct in their gloom-and-doom forecast, there'd be half a foot of snow on the ground already with more piling up. Vince could handle Tony, but if his wife

Linda called before Vince got in the car, he knew he'd have a *discussion* on his hands.

Triple H was sitting alone at a table while the catering guys wrapped up. It was clear that they wanted to get the hell out of Dodge, but no one got between Triple H and his postmatch meal. Triple H barely looked up when Vince approached, but he did kick a chair out for Vince to sit on. Vince waved the offered chair away. He didn't have time to stick around. "I'm on my way out, but I wanted to stop by to tell you a couple things."

"Yeah," Triple H said as he rested his fork on the plate and leaned back in his chair. Much as he and Vince had their problems from time to time, Hunter would not disrespect the man by eating through their conversation.

"First off, that was great shit. I mean, you guys tore the damn roof off this place."

"We did, didn't we?" Triple H said with a self-satisfied smile.

"I'm shocked you got out of there without a full security detail. Sounded like they wanted to rip your head off."

"Bring 'em on," Triple H said, and the two shared a laugh.

"I've got some ideas for what you and Austin can do next, but they're all . . . let's just say they're quite *involved."* Vince stressed that last word as a challenge, the implication being that he wasn't sure they could pull any of those ideas off. Vince knew this would be tantalizing enough to energize his WWE Champion. Few Superstars worked harder for the success of the company than Triple H. "When you and Austin get into the city tomorrow, we'll talk it over."

"Any reason we can't start talking about it now? Austin's still in the building. I can drag his ass in here. Give me two minutes."

Vince held up his hands, basically telling Triple H to back off. The truth was that Vince couldn't talk about the idea right now, because he didn't have the whole thing figured out yet. He was sure he would work it out eventually. "I'm running down to New York. I have that eight A.M. meeting with the network tomorrow and can't risk leaving in the morning with this weather. I should have been out of here hours ago, but wanted to watch the end of the show live. What you guys did will make the five-hour trip worth it."

"It's snowing like a bitch out there," Triple H said.

"I know. If anyone hears from Linda, tell her that I left here two hours ago."

Vince could hear Hunter laughing behind him as he walked away. Was getting in a car during a snowstorm the best idea Vince ever had? No. He knew that. But Vince gave the network folks his word he'd be there by eight, and he was determined to be there.

By the time Vince reached the arena exit, his car was waiting there for him, dug out and idling with Tony behind the wheel. Vince slipped into the backseat without waiting for Tony to get out and open the door for him. They had long since dispensed with that pretentious bit of business. Vince was perfectly capable of opening a door on his own.

It took them almost a half hour to fight their way out of the snow-covered parking lot past the crowds of people who had just watched Triple H reclaim his title. Vince knew that if any of them guessed he was behind the tinted windows of the town car, many of the fans would rush the car for his autograph, though probably more of them would pelt it with ice balls. He didn't mind. Their hatred for him was just one of the things that kept bringing them back.

By twelve-thirty they were slowly moving along the New York State Thruway. It had been tough negotiating the side roads, but the thruway was still passable, more or less.

Vince stared out the darkened windows. From the little he could see, he knew it was official—they were driving through a blizzard. Snow was falling or blowing around in every conceivable direction. The yellowish glow of the sporadic overhead road lights was the only reason Vince could see enough to know what was happening on the other side of the glass.

There was something about the swirling white storm that he found relaxing, and Vince allowed himself to shut down his mind and just enjoy the rare moment when people weren't pulling him in every direction. But right in the middle of thinking about *nothing,* both literal and figurative lightning flashed as he was struck by inspiration for what Triple H and Stone Cold could do the next night at the Garden.

But it was no lightning. And his inspiration wasn't the only thing that had been struck.

Tony managed to yell, "Hold on, Mister—" before Vince's head slammed against the window. The bright flash of light had faded, but he could sense the car was sliding down a hill. His own car's headlights were circling around him, so they must have been spinning. A warm taste ran over his lips. His head was bleeding. Vince hoped that was the worst of it. His stomach wobbled as the car began its third rotation, or maybe it was the fourth. He'd lost track. Cold air rushed in from the front passenger door as it flew open. The car finally slammed to a halt, sending Vince's left shoulder crashing into the glass partition between the passenger and driver.

Worse than the cut on his head or the searing pain

in his shoulder was the realization that the idea for Triple H's and Stone Cold's next match had left him. Gone. Just as quickly as it appeared. Before he could worry too much about that, he heard Tony calling out through the cracked glass partition. "Mister McMahon, are you okay?"

"More or less," Vince yelled back. He grabbed his briefcase and kicked his way out the driver's-side back door. "How 'bout you?"

"Yeah," Tony said as they met outside the car. The front end of the Lincoln was resting up against the tree it had slammed into. "I'm fine, sir. I am *so* sorry." His eyes went wide. "You're bleeding! Oh, God, I'm sorry! I didn't even see that snowplow. It came up on us so fast."

"Is that what it was?" Vince asked. "Damn crazy driver. Probably didn't even see us on the road. It wasn't your fault. Let's just be glad we're okay. This cut is nothing. Let's call nine-one-one and get out of here." Vince reached into his jacket pocket, pulled out his cell phone, and flipped it open. "Son of a bitch!"

"What's wrong, sir?"

"No service. Damn storm. Let's check your phone." No luck.

The two men stared at each other briefly. Vince could tell that Tony was afraid for his job. But firing

Tony was the furthest thing from Vince's mind. It wasn't his fault.

"Suggestions?" Vince asked. Other than the snow-plow, they hadn't seen another car in the past twenty minutes. Waiting it out by the side of the road seemed foolhardy.

"Well," Tony began, sounding about as confident as the captain of the chess team asking the head cheerleader to the prom. "I saw a diner about a mile back, right off the exit. We can probably get there in twenty minutes."

"Let's go," Vince said as he started walking. He didn't give a damn if the diner was open or not. They'd probably have a pay phone he could use to call for help. Moving was a much better option than sitting around freezing their asses off in the snow.

The two men hardly spoke during the trek. With the freezing air it was just easier to keep their jaws clenched and walk. It took longer than Tony said it would, but Vince was downright shocked when they shuffled down to the end of the exit ramp. Visible through the driving white abyss was a glowing bill-board with the words "Whirlybird Diner" written across it in bold letters. Hanging beneath it, all lit up in bright neon red, was the only word Vince cared about right now: "OPEN."

As soon as they were inside the relative warmth

of the diner, Tony stepped right to the counter and struck up a conversation with the waitress. Vince stood a moment inside of the doorway to look around. He wanted to make sure his feet were actually on the diner's outdated linoleum and no longer out in the arctic. The warm air felt nice, but he knew that in a few minutes, once the numbness melted away, his head would be throbbing.

Vince took stock of the place. Bunch of beat-up chrome stools with fake leather tops that probably didn't spin around anymore, that is, if they ever did. Across the counter from the stools were refrigerator cases holding desserts that did not appear to be made today. Or this week. As he continued his inventory, Vince settled on something he couldn't believe was in front of him—another patron. The man sat in the booth farthest from the door, facing away from him. Vince figured the dive was the only option for people stuck out on the road in the middle of the night.

"Good news, Mister McMahon, the coffee's hot," Tony said as he turned to his boss.

"And the food's even hotter," said the waitress. "Or it will be once I get the grill up and running again. Been havin' a hell of a time keeping it goin' with that storm outside."

"You the cook too?" Vince asked.

"Cook, waitress, hostess, busboy . . . you name it." She flashed him a yellowed smile. "What can I get you?"

"A phone," Vince said.

"Over there," she said, pointing to the far end of the diner. "But it won't help. Ice snapped the phone lines. Nobody'll be out till morning to fix 'em. And the hotel up the street is already booked solid."

"Christ," Vince spat. "You have any good news?"

"Just that hot food," she said. "If sweetie here will help me out."

Tony looked to Vince for what to do. Vince nodded. He might as well get something warm in him. It looked like they were going to be there a while. While Tony went in back with the waitress, Vince figured he might as well make himself comfortable. No point being rude either, since it looked like one other weary traveler was in the same boat.

"Hell of a night," Vince said to the gray-haired man at the end of the diner. The man simply nodded in agreement without turning around. That was odd. Not to mention rude. But Vince was undaunted. "Had to get to the city, or else I would've stayed up in Albany myself. What about you?"

The guy shrugged in response as Vince ambled up to him. Vince did his best to keep his anger in check, seeing as how they were stuck together. Still, he wasn't used to people ignoring him. The chairman of the WWE did not get treated like this.

"Hey, buddy," Vince said as he reached the guy. "What's your—" Vince froze colder than the air outside. He couldn't have been more shocked by what he saw than if someone had told him Hulk Hogan had actually retired once and for all. "Phil? Phil Thompson?"

The man in the booth gave Vince a smirk and nodded to the bench across from him. "Have a seat, Vince."

It had been over forty years since Vince had last seen the man in front of him. It was nice to see that the years had been harder on Thompson than they had on Vince. In spite of the changes, the recognition was instant. Thompson's gray hair was cropped in the tight style of their youth. His face showed a few wrinkles—and a few more scars. Vince only wished he had been the cause of some of those scars.

"You going to stand there all night?" Phil said. " 'Cause I don't know how long Rita is going to be able to keep your friend busy with that grill."

Vince did not like this at all. Running into an old enemy in the middle of a snowstorm in the middle of the night. Something was not right.

"What the hell are you doing here?" Vince asked.

"Like seeing a ghost, isn't it?" Thompson replied. "What's it been . . . thirty, forty years?"

Vince was in no mood for small talk. "Look, Thompson, I don't know what you want . . ."

Thompson jumped in. "Not much. Just to share a cup of coffee with an old friend."

"We were never friends."

"A technicality," Thompson said glibly. "In a different time at a different place . . ."

"You still would have been the same asshole."

Thompson didn't even bother to look offended. "You're probably right," he said. "But look at you now. I can't say I'm an avid fan, but I keep up on you and tune into *Raw* and *SmackDown!* when I have a chance. I'm real happy for you. Things turned out real well."

"No thanks to you."

"Now don't tell me you still hold a grudge."

Vince was tired of standing and just a bit woozy from his head injury. He slid into the seat across from Thompson. "You've seen me on TV. You tell me if I can't hold a grudge."

"Still, forty years is a long time to hate someone."

"I've hated people longer," Vince said.

Thompson checked his watch. "This isn't quite going the way I planned. I was hoping you would have gotten here sooner. But I can see how you'd be running late, considering the weather and all."

"Late?" Vince said, his anger rising. "We weren't

planning on stopping here. We were an accident. Some asshole plow driver ran us off the road."

"Technically, yes, you did have a car wreck, but it was not an *accident*. Although the severity of the crash wasn't supposed to be near what it was. I should have known it might get out of hand. Ice can be so . . . unpredictable."

"You bastard!" Vince reached across the table and grabbed Thompson by the collar. "You did this?!"

"Please," Thompson asked as his face went red. "Just give me five minutes. You will understand all of this. Why I'm here. Why we did what we did. Vince . . . your country needs your help."

"First of all, what the hell are you talking about?" Vince fumed, but refused to let go of his grip. "And secondly, I already give this country a lot of help. I pay my taxes—all of my taxes—on time, I send my Superstars out to entertain the troops, and I've made more than my fair share of monetary contributions to the current administration."

"We know," Thompson said, causing Vince to wonder about this "we" that his old acquaintance was referring to. "Which is part of the reason we thought you'd be approachable. Part of you wants to know why we've arranged all this, am I right?"

"You've got five minutes," Vince said as he released Thompson.

"I've changed since our days at the Academy," Phil said. "And I owe a lot of that to you."

"Flowers are a better way to show your appreciation than car accidents," Vince said. "Stop buttering me up and make your damn point."

"You'll probably be surprised to know that I'm now director of the NSA," he said.

"Not at all," Vince said. "You were always a conniving, backstabbing bastard. I had no doubt you'd go far."

Thompson ignored the attitude, but cut to the chase. "Since nine-eleven, the NSA's ability to handle situations has gotten more, let's just say, more . . . liberal. But it's still not enough. We're fighting too much from too many directions. We need help."

Well, that answered the question of "who." Now all Vince needed to know was "what."

Thompson continued, "You, Vince, are the chairman of a company that travels all over the country, all over the world really. Every week. Strong men and women. Patriots, all of them. With more physical abilities than most of our operatives."

"Yeah, I'm damned proud of them too," Vince said. "Four minutes."

"They could be just the help the NSA has been searching for," Thompson said. "The Superstars of WWE storm into a town one night and move on to another the next. You travel with truckloads of equipment like you're your own damn mobile city. With people and resources that match any force the government has at our disposal."

"You're not using my Superstars as decoys, if that's what you want. So don't even bother asking."

"No, no. You think I'm going to tell Triple H, 'I know you can snap a man's neck in two seconds, but wait right here where someone can take a shot at you so we can arrest him.' Give me a break. I deserve more credit than that. I want them to be involved."

Even though Vince hadn't seen Thompson in about forty years, he could tell the guy was holding back. *Screw the time limit.* "Great seeing you," Vince said with a sneer. "Maybe we'll run into one another again in, I don't know, forty years."

"You're not getting this, are you?" Thompson's entire demeanor changed. He had been serious for the entire time they talked, but now something else was bubbling to the surface. It wasn't quite anger. More like frustration. "Let me topline it. We set up a handful of Superstars as a special operations force. My guys identify the problem. Your guys go in and clean it up. Job done. You pack up your trucks and move on to the next city. No one's the wiser."

"Case you haven't noticed, my guys tend to attract some attention when they go out," Vince said.

"We use that in our favor when we can," Phil said. "Work around it when we can't."

"And they'd be on the government's payroll?"

"A discretionary fund," Phil said. "Purely black ops."

"You think I'm an idiot?" Vince asked, getting up from the table. "I've seen movies. I watch TV. You suddenly show up after forty years with this ridiculous offer, sweet-talk me into it, get my guys working for you and all. Then bam! A few years down the line we find out you're the bad guy and we've been working against our own government. Sorry, buddy. I'm nobody's fool. Least of all yours."

"Wait, Vince," Thompson said, grabbing Vince by the arm.

Vince looked down, seething.

Thompson quickly released him. "Wait," he pleaded. "If I can't convince you, I know someone who can." Phil opened up his briefcase and took out a laptop. He raised the screen and tapped a few keys. "Just give me a second to make the connection. . . . Here we go."

Phil slid the computer out so that Vince could see the screen. It was black, except for the word

big apple takedown

CONNECTING flashing in white letters. Vince couldn't wait to see what kind of crap Thompson was going to pull now. Luckily, he didn't have to wait for long. After a few seconds of nothingness, the screen switched to a frozen image.

It was the seal of the president of the United States.

chapter
one

Two years later . . .

Hunter Hearst Helmsley adjusted his ill-fitting thick-framed glasses and pounded down the last of his beer. Vince would be pissed if he knew Triple H was drinking while on assignment, but it wasn't like one beer was going to impair his abilities or anything. He was still a long way away from being even slightly buzzed. The waitress sauntered over to the table with the offer of another, but Hunter refused. He didn't want to look bad in front of a potential employer. Hunter allowed himself a slight chuckle. Like he needed to worry about this job interview. Aside from the fact that he had a pretty cush job already—two, in fact—it wasn't like there was any doubt he'd be hired. Well, maybe a little, but he wasn't concerned.

Hunter checked his watch. His appointment was fifteen minutes late. *I guess you can't count on the criminal element to keep to a schedule.* The only annoying part about the wait was, the waitress kept watching him. At first he thought she recognized him as the Cerebral Assassin. Even with his slicked-back hair tied into a ponytail and the damn glasses, it was hard to hide his pure size. But it was more likely that the waitress was just bored. He *was* her only customer.

He wasn't surprised that the bar was empty. It wasn't even noon yet. Though Hunter knew the bars in this part of Brooklyn probably saw action from opening to closing, he wasn't complaining that he was alone. The patrons in this part of town were his kind of people. And, more importantly, he was their kind of celebrity. This wouldn't be the first time he was undercover in a place where he risked being recognized. But far from worrying him, it just added to the fun.

The front door opened, letting the streaming light

of day into the darkened bar. Hunter wasn't sure if his contact was coming in or not. The guy was back-lit by the sun. The one thing Hunter could tell was that the guy wasn't alone. Once the door shut and everyone adjusted to the light, Hunter saw that it was time to get down to business. He threw up a hand in a wave and motioned for his contact to come over to his table.

Trent Gorman saw Hunter's hand. A look of relief mixed with no small amount of visible fear washed over him as he stumbled over his own feet getting to the table. The man beside Trent did not seem amused. Hunter wasn't either. At the moment, his life was in this guy's hands. Trent needed to get his act together.

Hunter stood to greet the new arrivals. Those kinds of manners probably weren't seen much in this bar, but Hunter wasn't playing to the waitress and bartender. His mark was all that he cared to impress.

"Sorry we're late, *Mike,*" Trent said as he shook Hunter's hand. "Work's been a little busy lately."

"Sounds like you need me," Hunter said, playing the role of Mike.

"We'll see about that," Trent's friend replied.

"Mike Landon"—Trent nodded to Hunter, addressing him by his alias—"meet Garrett Fischer."

The two men exchanged greetings and shook

hands. Hunter was amused by the excessively strong grip Fischer forced on him in an attempt to assert dominance. Hunter knew he could crush the guy's hand if he wanted to, but that would be counter-productive.

Even more amusing was how the guy looked. It must have cost Fischer a lot of money for him to look that tacky. Aside from the ill-fitting suit and the highly styled hair, the spray-painted tan he was sporting looked like it was running in places. His poor attempt at a show of wealth only served to make him stand out like a sore thumb in this part of town. It wasn't exactly the way to go unnoticed, considering his line of work.

"Have a seat," Hunter said.

Trent slid into the opposite side of the booth, leaving the outer seat for Fischer. As soon as his ass hit the vinyl, the waitress was hovering over them. "What can I get ya?" she asked. The waitress had directed the question to Trent first, but he looked at Fischer as if asking permission to order.

"It's a bit early for alcohol," Fischer said to the waitress. "Just give me a soda water with a twist of lime."

"I'll have the same," Trent quickly jumped in.

The waitress looked at Hunter. "Gimme another Amstel," he said, not bothering to play follow-the-leader. He could tell that Fischer appreciated that devil-may-care attitude, as opposed to Trent's lack of independence.

"So, Mike, Trent here says you're the kind of guy my operation needs. Are you?" Fischer asked bluntly.

Hunter was surprised the guy got right to business. First impression alone indicated that Fischer wasn't much of an entrepreneur. "Depends on what you're looking for," Hunter said.

"Why don't you impress me with your qualifications?"

Hunter ran down his cover story. "Four years at Green Haven Correctional for money laundering. Five at Mid-Orange for drug trafficking. Twenty at Sullivan for manslaughter. Oh, and a year at Riker's for assault."

Fischer was clearly doing some quick calculations in his head. "So you're telling me you've been in jail since you were . . . six?"

"No, I'm telling you what I would have been in for if I was ever caught," Hunter said as the waitress arrived with their drinks. He grabbed the glass before it hit the table and took a swig to punctuate his résumé.

"And I'm supposed to be impressed by your arrogance?" Fischer asked.

"Just answering your question. If that's not enough, I'd be happy to supply references," Hunter said as he put down the glass. "Though most of my former employers are relaxing on beaches in countries with more accessible banking and less stringent extradition laws."

Fischer cracked a smile. "Arrogance with a touch of humor. I like that. So what has Trent here told you I need?"

"Someone to handle your crew," Hunter said. "Hiring, firing, *permanent* relocation, that sort of thing."

"In a nutshell," Fischer said. "I'm sure he's also told you we've recently been . . . expanding our business opportunities, opening up our market."

"Thought I might like to get in on the ground floor," Hunter said, flashing Trent an appreciative smile that he hoped would calm the guy down a bit. Hunter could feel Trent's leg shaking so hard, the floor beneath them was vibrating.

"Since our Nervous Nellie here vouched for you, I'm willing to give it a try." Fischer smacked Trent on the arm and leaned in. "Don't worry. Your guy's impressed me so far." He turned to Hunter. "Want to check out the operation, Mike?"

"Looking forward to it."

Fischer waved the waitress over and settled up their tab. When they were back outside, Fischer suggested that Trent ride with "Mike" to what they called "headquarters." Since Hunter had only a beer and three sips, he was perfectly fine to drive. He walked down the street to his loaner SUV and got in.

"Calm down, man," Hunter said as Trent slipped into the passenger seat. "It's cool. Nothing to worry about."

"I don't think I can do this," Trent said. His leg was shaking so violently that the SUV was rocking.

"I'm in," Hunter said. "Your job is done. All you gotta do now is go along for the ride." He started up the SUV and followed Fischer's shiny Lexus through the Brooklyn streets. Thankfully Trent had stopped whining about his role in this plan. Hunter had no interest in playing babysitter. He knew it was a bad idea from the start. Any guy who turns on his boss out of fear isn't going to be that reliable a source to begin with. Hunter was hanging an awful lot of faith on the fact that Trent was supposed to get him in with Fischer and stay cool enough to let Hunter get the job done.

Hunter kept his eyes on the car in front of him so Fischer didn't lose him. It didn't matter, since Trent knew where they were going, but Hunter didn't think Fischer would be all that impressed if his new hire couldn't manage a simple task like follow-the-leader. Not that Fischer was making it any easier on him, the way he blew through stop signs and careened around corners, screeching with every turn. Hunter was shocked that the guy hadn't been caught sooner. He wasn't exactly hard to find.

Since Hunter had no interest in starting up another conversation with Trent, he occupied himself with going over the facts of the case in his mind. According to the files, Garret Fischer had been a criminal before he entered junior high. As an eleven-year-old, he took a baseball bat to another kid's head to end a disagreement on balls and strikes and never looked back. Grand theft auto, drug running, interstate transportation of stolen goods—the list went on.

For all he'd done, Fischer only had a few stints in lockup. That wasn't much of a surprise, having met the man. He didn't exactly scream low-profile. Hunter had taken a risk in playing up the fact that "Mike" had never been caught. He was trusting that Fischer would want someone more talented than himself keeping watch over his organization. It would be a balancing act for Hunter to continue impressing his new boss without becoming a threat.

Fischer now ran a methamphetamine empire out of a warehouse somewhere in Brooklyn. The fact that the NSA couldn't come up with a location until they managed to turn Trent Gorman had sent up a red flag for Hunter when he was first assigned the mission. The fact that he was following a speeding, screeching *Lexus* to that warehouse confirmed his initial suspicion: the NSA hadn't been giving Fischer the least amount of priority.

True, Brooklyn had been growing considerably more upscale in recent years. Chic restaurants were springing up in Red Hook. Williamsburg had gotten so popular with the old downtown hipster crowd that it was already a cliché. The artists were taking over Park Slope, and with them came fashionable boutiques and coffee shops with open mike nights and poetry slams. So a Lexus tooling around along the city streets would not stand out. A Lexus heading in and out of the warehouse district on a daily basis? That was a different matter entirely.

Sections of Brooklyn were stuck still in the pre-Giuliani early 1990s, patches here and there where violent crime didn't have the 80 percent decrease the police commissioner so often liked to talk about. Fischer had apparently found one of these patches, set up shop a few months ago, and made boatloads of money poisoning people's minds.

Synthetic methamphetamines were Fischer's particular brand of poison. At first, Hunter didn't take the assignment seriously. It made no sense to him that the NSA would be interested in some drug lab that made a product you could easily get anywhere from run-down drug houses on skid row to the upscale neighborhoods in the suburbs, where it was cooked up by bored housewives. But that was where Fischer *did* interest the government. His product wasn't simply being sold on the street. He was using top-of-the-line ingredients to create a mixture of meth that was shipping out across the country and flying off the proverbial shelves. It was a surprisingly big-time operation for a relatively small-time hood.

When the two cars pulled up in front of the beat-up warehouse in the Decatur section of Brooklyn, Hunter briefly reevaluated his opinion of the NSA's surveillance. This did not look like the kind of place that would house a major illegal drug operation.

The oversized warehouse was rusted-out and run-down. It looked as if it had been abandoned for decades. The only thing the place seemed to have going for it was its size. It was huge. A smaller annex building attached to the side added to its enormity, but that too looked as though it had seen better days. The seemingly ancient compound was surrounded by rusted-out trailers and rail cars the city no longer used. A tenement building that hadn't been lawfully inhabited in at least twenty years rose behind the building. The front of the warehouse was open to the world along, with about a half block of weeded-up, cracked, and peeling blacktop in front of it.

"Leave your cell phone here," Trent said as they pulled up. "Or someone will just take it from you inside."

"I don't think so," Hunter said. "I need an out if we run into trouble."

Trent shook his head. "Won't do you any good in there anyway. All cell signals are blocked. Nothing gets in or out except the land line in the security booth."

Hunter looked back at the warehouse. It seemed incredibly run-down to house anything so hi-tech. Reluctantly, he dropped his cell phone into the cup holder and got out of the SUV.

"Nice place you got here," Hunter said with a twinge of skepticism in his voice as Fischer hopped out of his car with a shit-eating grin on his face. It was the kind of look that Hunter read as "you'll see."

The only visible way into the building was a door front and center, a few feet away from a ramp leading up to a loading dock with a huge metal roll-up door. Hunter followed Fischer in a three-person parade that looked just as out of place as the Lexus in front of the beat-up old warehouse.

As they reached the door, Hunter leaned in slightly to see what Fischer was doing and was rewarded with the first sign that all was not as it seemed. The rusted old door did not have a matching rusted old lock. In fact, it didn't seem to have a standard lock at all. Fischer held a plastic access card up to a black box beside the door. Hunter heard a click as the lock mechanism turned inside the walls. He looked up and saw a surveillance camera trained on the entrance, keeping record of everyone coming in and out. He doubted that it was the only camera in the area.

The next sign that something was a little off came when Hunter grabbed the door from Fischer as he walked inside. From the outside, it looked like a thin metal door, so rusted and old that it would snap in a slight breeze. In his hand he felt the heft of the thing, which had obviously been reinforced with steel.

Once inside, Hunter found himself in a small covered entryway. He could see into the warehouse, but a tall black man was standing on the other side, blocking him from getting a full view of the place.

"Empty your pockets," Fischer said as he handed Hunter a small bowl like the ones they had at airport security screening stations. Hunter dropped his keys into the bowl and handed it to Fischer, who handed it to the man on the other side. The guy took a close look at the keys. It was doubtful he would notice anything about the keychain, but Hunter said a silent prayer to whatever god might be watching that the guy didn't inspect it too closely. Hunter decided to keep his glasses on, but he adjusted them on his face, taking hold of them behind the ear and squeezing the end.

The man inside the warehouse pressed a button on the side of the entryway. A bright red light flashed and scanned up and down Hunter's body. He assumed it was some X-ray type device that could pick up any weapons or transmitting devices, which would make it hard to get any kind of bugging equipment in later.

That settles it, Hunter thought. *This is way too advanced an operation for what it said in the files about Fischer.*

chapter
two

"Sorry," Fischer said as the red light swept over them. "Security precaution." He directed his attention to a panel on the side of the small room. Once the beam completed its sweep, a green light came on.

"All clear," the black guy said.

"If you're trying to impress me, you're doing a good job," Hunter said to Fischer as his keys were handed back to him.

"As the saying goes, you ain't seen nothing yet." Fisher beamed with self-satisfied pride as he ushered Hunter inside. Hunter almost couldn't blame the guy. From the outside it was the best example of urban blight Hunter had ever seen. But inside was a fully functioning operation the likes of which he had not seen since he started working with the NSA.

The only thing seeing the outside of the warehouse had prepared him for was the massive size of the place. It was huge. But the worn and rusted exterior did not match the modern functioning interior that he saw once he crossed the threshold into the building. More than just given a fresh coat of paint, the place had obviously been gutted and reinforced. The warehouse had been split down the middle, with storage on the right—rows and rows of boxes stacked up to twice Hunter's height. The left side was taken over by what was clearly new construction. A separate building had been created inside the warehouse, closing the space off from the rest of the place. Even though there weren't any windows to allow him to see inside the smaller building, Hunter had no doubt that it was the lab. A series of small offices had been built along the wall opposite the lab. There was also a large archway in that wall that looked like it went out to the annex building. Hunter could see some metal barrels by the entrance to that space. It was, quite frankly, overwhelming.

A half-dozen men were carrying various boxes out of a back room and carefully stacking them in piles by the loading bay door off to the side of the security entrance. The men apparently took their jobs very seriously, as they weren't even bothering to shoot the shit as they moved. Each and every one of them stepped up their work when they saw the boss had arrived.

"Preparing your stock for a move?" Hunter asked. "Have to say, it looks like the situation is under control." The men were moving in and out of the back room with ease. Hunter assumed that was the actual "lab" part of the meth lab operation, but he couldn't see inside from his current vantage point. There was no need to rush, though. He'd have the chance to explore soon enough.

"We move things out on a weekly basis," Fischer said. "Outgoing isn't the problem. We've got that handled fine. It's getting the ingredients in where I need the help. I'm afraid our monthly materials changeover is a bit too much for Trent here to handle on his own."

"That's why I suggested Mike, Mister Fischer," Trent said nervously. "He's got a lot of experience with moving things without bringing too much attention to himself. He knows all about that kind of stuff."

"Tell me about your operation," Hunter said as he adjusted his glasses again and took in the entire space. "I need to know how you work if I'm gonna figure out what needs to change."

Fischer motioned for Hunter to follow as he started walking to his office. "My employees come and go in the dark. When they're scheduled to work, they work a twenty-four-hour shift starting at midnight. That way we keep the traffic to the middle of the night. We got parking set up down the block so there's nothing to tie them here. During a shift the guys are four hours on, two hours off, so they don't start making mistakes. We got cots in back for resting. So it's twenty-four hours on, twenty-four hours off, and back to work. Of course, senior management like us can come and go as we please.

"There are no phones allowed in here. No recording equipment of any kind inside the building. The surveillance cameras you'll see are all live to the security booth. Nothing is being recorded. We don't need to provide evidence in the unlikely event we get caught. Of course, if you try to bring anything—even a cell phone—inside, you wouldn't get past the front door. We take our security very seriously here. That was Ray, my security chief, who met us at the door. Should've introduced you, now that I think of it. Ah, well, you'll meet him later." Fischer ended his speech sitting in the plush leather chair behind his glass and chrome desk. Nothing in the modernized warehouse looked nearly as out of place as the office furniture.

Hunter took stock of the room, careful to notice anything that could be of use. It wasn't a difficult task. The glass desktop was empty except for the laptop that sat open, facing Fischer. The desk itself was little more than a tabletop, with no drawers, no place to hold information. There wasn't even a filing cabinet in the room. Hunter noticed a wireless router plugged into the wall, but that was about it for contents of the room. It was ridiculously bare.

Hunter remained standing as he considered what Fischer had told him. "It's an okay system. And you got a great location, but there is some room for improvement," he said. "First thing you want to do is stagger start times for the workers. No point in having everyone coming and going in the middle of the night if they're doing it in clumps. No more than two in and two out of the building at any time. I'm going to need to have a more flexible schedule to get things I need from my outside sources, so that management part is fine with me. But you might want to consider parking down the block yourself, 'cause nothing sticks out more than a Lexus in this neighborhood."

"Oh, Ray's gonna love you," Fischer said. "He's always on my ass about security."

"So when do you need me to start?" Hunter asked.

"I like that," Fischer said. "Most people would wait for me to offer them the job first."

"Trent seemed to think you needed someone right away," Hunter said. "But if you've got time to dick around . . ." Hunter could see Trent visibly tense beside him. No wonder the NSA couldn't trust this guy to be a mole on his own. He'd never be able to pull it off.

"Careful," Fischer said, lightly. "You don't want to go pissing off your boss before you even start."

"So, I'm hired?"

"Would I have taken you back here if you weren't?"

Hunter wanted to say, "Yes, you probably would," but he chose to remain silent. Pointing out Fischer's pathetic excuse for personal security was counterproductive to Hunter's mission. Besides, the guy probably wouldn't listen anyway.

The room began to flash with red light as a klaxon sounded. Hunter stiffened and readied himself for an attack. Fischer saw the concern in Hunter's eyes. "Looks like we've got a visitor," he calmly explained. "I'm afraid I had to blow off a meeting to get together with you."

Hunter just nodded as he turned his attention to the front entrance. Ray had bolted out of the security booth, but slowed considerably once he saw the man coming through the entryway. It was a very tall, very blond, *very* well dressed man who Fischer had clearly been trying to imitate with his own wardrobe choices. However, where Fischer failed in his flashy, gaudy look, this man succeeded with his fine fabrics and polished looks.

The mystery man was flanked by two bodyguards who looked like they came straight out of a James Bond movie. The first one was a tall white guy with a buzz cut and a tattoo running down the right side of his face. The other guy was an equally large black man with excessive amounts of silver jewelry. Together, the three of them had just strolled through the security entrance without bothering to stop for a scan.

At least Hunter now knew what would happen if he tried to bring in any equipment from the outside world. The man seemed oblivious to the noise, as if he couldn't even hear it. Either that, or he just didn't give a damn that he was the cause. The latter seemed far more likely. Hunter watched as Ray turned around and headed back into the booth. A moment later the klaxon went silent, and the red light stopped flashing.

"Fischer," the man said as he barged his way into the office. "I do not like to be kept waiting."

"Sorry, man," Fischer said, not sounding regretful in the least. "But I think I found the guy to help with the move." He nodded toward Hunter, who was intrigued by this new player. All his paperwork had indicated that Fischer was the top man. But nobody wearing the stranger's style of suit reported to anyone the likes of Fischer. At least it explained why the setup for this operation seemed so far out of Fischer's league.

"Mike Landon," Hunter said, holding out a hand. The stranger did not reach for it, nor return the greeting. He just looked at Fischer. "I need to speak to you. Now."

"Certainly," Fischer said. "Mike, why don't you come back tomorrow? Trent, could you show him out?"

"Yes, sir," Trent said as he quickly fled the office. Hunter wanted to stay behind to listen in, but knew that wouldn't go over so well.

"Who's the guy?" Hunter asked Trent after the office door was closed behind them.

"I don't know," Trent said in a hushed voice so no one overheard. "I've only seen him a coupla times. Do you think he's important?"

"Well, *he* certainly thinks he is," Hunter said. Trent said his good-byes before he had to go through the security door. The alarms and lights had been reset, but Hunter didn't want to give any reason for them to go off again. He adjusted his glasses once again and went outside, blinking back the bright sunlight as he walked to his SUV.

He paused to look over the area. The stranger's town car was parked off to the side. Hunter subtly checked out the license plate, but he didn't want to be caught staring. He could see the outline of the driver watching him from behind the wheel. Not wanting to attract too much attention, Hunter got into the SUV and drove off. Once he was a few blocks away, he pulled to the side of the road and pushed a button on the GPS system. The screen blinked on, and the words BEGIN TRANSMISSION appeared.

Hunter removed his glasses, glad to finally get them off his face. They were much more uncomfortable than they appeared, which probably had something to do with the fact that the genius who made them never bothered to properly fit them to Hunter's face. Hunter reached into the cup holder beside him, removed his cell phone, and slipped aside the bottom panel where the cup would rest if he had one. From the compartment beneath he pulled out two wires with metal clips on the end. He hooked a clip on each end of the arms of the glasses and laid them to rest in the cup holder. Once the GPS screen read TRANSMITTING, Hunter pulled the car back onto the road. It was time to get back to Manhattan.

chapter
three

Triple H dropped his duffel bag in his room before heading back to the elevator. He knew he was running late, but he honestly didn't care. He had been starving by the time he got back into the city, so he took a quick pit stop on the way to the hotel. After combing all that product crap out of his hair and doing a quick change in the SUV, he grabbed a bite at a restaurant in Hell's Kitchen. After a few autographs and a hot meal, Hunter hit the hotel for his post-mission brief.

The elevator doors opened up on the third floor, leaving Hunter face-to-face with Randy Orton.

"Hey, man," Randy said. "If you're here for the fitness center, don't bother. It's closed for renovation. We got to go down to the gym the office rented out for us."

"Man, that sucks," Hunter said as he got out of the elevator anyway. "Maybe someone there can open up the steam room or something. Still got that sore shoulder from the last show."

Randy shrugged. "Suit yourself."

Hunter watched as Randy hit the button for the lobby and the elevator doors closed in front of him. That done, he continued down the hall to the hotel spa. The glass doors did, in fact, have a small sign on them announcing the renovation closure and apologizing for the inconvenience. Hunter ignored the sign, opened the doors, and stepped into the soothingly green-and-beige waiting room. A receptionist wearing a polo shirt that matched the walls sat working at a computer. He was so focused on his work that Hunter wasn't sure that the guy knew he was there. Hunter cleared his throat.

"Sorry, we're—" The receptionist looked up pleasantly, until he saw who was in front of him. That's when the smile faded and the pleasant hotel employee attitude was dropped. "Oh, it's you. You're late."

"Good to see you too," Hunter said. "Where's Thompson?"

"He went out for coffee," the receptionist said with an actual sneer. "Wasn't going to wait around all day for you."

"He got the download?"

"Two hours ago."

Hunter didn't miss the lack of subtlety in the guy's tone. He didn't give a damn about it either. Hunter leaned down, towering over the receptionist, causing him to lose that sneer. "Tell him I'm in my room when he gets back."

"No need to intimidate the staff," a voice said from behind Hunter. "I'm here."

Hunter turned to see Phil Thompson standing in the doorway, holding a steaming cup of Starbucks' finest. "The video turn out okay?"

"Perfect," Thompson said. "You did a great job. Really first-rate. You handled those video-camera glasses like a pro."

Hunter felt the guy was pouring it on a bit thick for what amounted to about a half hour of work. Though he was still relatively new to the espionage game, Hunter had been working with Phil long enough to be suspicious. "You got a good image off the recording, right? A shot of that guy in the *fancy* suit?"

"Yes," Thompson said as he closed the distance between him and Hunter. "About that. Why don't you come in back with me?"

Now Hunter knew something was wrong. The complimentary snow job was one thing, but Thompson never had a problem talking about stuff in front of his flunky before. "Spill it," Hunter said, refusing to budge.

Thompson looked at the prissy guy at the computer, who suddenly found whatever was on the screen to be *very* interesting. "As you know," he said, "we were hoping to find an explanation for how Garrett Fischer became such a major player in the drug trade so quickly."

"I remember the assignment."

"The video you obtained gave us an answer," Thompson said. "The gentleman in the fancy suit is someone we've been after for a very long time."

"Great," Hunter said. "I'll be sure to warm up to him next time he comes by." Hunter could swear he heard the receptionist snicker.

"Yes," Thompson said, in a way that made Hunter think, No. The NSA director looked down at the receptionist, then back at Hunter. "The gentleman is a very powerful player. I'm afraid we're going to need to bring some of our more highly trained operatives into play. Please understand it's nothing personal. You did a great job with the video. It's just, we can't risk losing this lead."

"And you think taking me out of play and suddenly dropping someone else in the mix won't look suspicious? According to the mission brief you gave me, Trent said something big was about to go down. Fischer basically told me the same thing when I met him. This is not time to start playing games."

"It's an acceptable risk," Thompson said. "This is not a one-man operation."

"So don't use one man," Hunter said, his anger starting to boil. "I know you've recruited other Superstars. Any idiot could figure that out. Vince didn't just come to me. For whatever reason, you don't want us knowing about each other. Well, now we're here, all in one place, and it looks to me like you can use us. So use us."

"It's not that easy," Thompson said.

"Oh, yes it is," came the gravelly voice of Vince McMahon.

Both men turned to find the chairman of the WWE entering the reception area. Hunter found it interesting that Vince wasn't coming from the hall. He was coming from the spa itself, like he had been waiting there for them. And he certainly didn't look like he had been having a relaxing seaweed wrap. Hunter caught Thompson shooting a look at the receptionist, who replied with a shrug and a "Don't look at me" expression.

"Slipped in while your guy was at lunch," Vince

said, explaining his surprise entrance to the NSA director. "I thought you might pull something like this when I saw how you looked when you saw that guy on the screen earlier. When you were out, I ran his face through the image recognition software. Crazy what computers can do these days, isn't it?"

"Then you know he's too important to entrust to a lone operative," Thompson said.

"I agree," Vince replied. Hunter started to object, but Vince held up a hand. "Come with me."

Curious, Hunter followed his boss without waiting to see if Thompson came along too. He did. In fact, Hunter half expected the guy behind the reception desk to come along as well. Vince McMahon certainly knew how to build up anticipation.

The three men walked down the green-and-beige hall, past all the massage rooms, the tanning beds, and the sauna, ending up in the actual gym. Hunter wasn't entirely amazed by what he saw when he got there. He was almost expecting them to be there. But he still hadn't been prepared for *who*.

Looking just as confused as Hunter felt were John Cena, Chavo Guerrero, Batista, and Torrie Wilson.

chapter
four

The WWE Superstars were scattered about the room, sitting on various pieces of exercise equipment. Apparently, the desk jockey up front had been away from his post for some time, if they had all got in without him noticing.

Hunter was surprised to see the other Superstars. He had spent so much time wondering who else Vince and the NSA had tagged as operatives that it was especially shocking to learn the truth. He had pretty much assumed Cena was working for the NSA. That guy had his finger in everything lately. But the rest of them were unexpected. Hunter couldn't wait to see how this turned out.

That is, if Phil Thompson would allow it.

"No way," Thompson said as he came in behind Hunter and saw the other Superstars in the room. "Having these operatives in one room at the same time is already a major breach of protocol. I cannot do what you are suggesting."

"Yes, you can," Vince said simply. "And if you want to continue working with my people, you will."

Hunter didn't need to rely on his training on reading subjects to know that something beyond a simple disagreement was going on. Ever since Hunter was first recruited, he had suspected that the story Vince told him about himself and Phil being old school chums was a load of crap. There was something about the way Vince looked when he talked about Phil. He always looked pissed, even when giving the guy a compliment. Vince held some kind of power over his old friend, as far as Hunter could tell. It showed in a look the men exchanged in the few times Hunter had seen Vince challenge the NSA director. Hunter saw that look now. Vince was the kind of person who made sure he held the power in any given situation, whether it was a board meeting with WWE upper management or simply drinks with the guys. Vince was the man in charge, even when he wasn't the one with the title. It was that way right now.

Thompson shook his head, giving the first indication that he was about to give in. "I can't get clearance for this."

"Get it," Vince said simply.

"Can we have a word, please?" Thompson asked.

"No."

Hunter would have called it an impasse, but it wasn't really. Vince was going to get what he wanted. Many other guys would have tried to force the issue with Vince, but not Phil. He just went into the spa office—which he had claimed for his own—and made a call. Once he left the room, Hunter was able to focus again on the fact that he was not the lone Superstar at the meeting. Sure, he had known other guys had been recruited, but the reality of seeing them in front of him was especially rewarding after all this time.

Vince addressed his Superstars as soon as Thompson was out of the room. "I know you have a ton of questions, but we don't have time for them. As has been made abundantly clear, we've stumbled onto something the NSA hadn't anticipated. I know Thompson is going to brief you about the mission when he comes out of that little room, so I'll leave that to him. In the meantime, let me bring you up to speed about yourselves.

"Triple H has been in the program the longest. Since this is his mission to begin with, he'll be in

charge. He's been primarily involved in border issues, closing down small-time operations bringing
contraband into the country through Canada. Torrie
and John have worked together before. In fact,
they're the only ones among you that have been
paired up for a mission. Together, they busted a sex
slave ring in suburban Chicago. Chavo has run a
couple missions targeting Internet hackers. Unfortunately, most of his work has resulted in the arrests of
teenage boys, which, as you know, cuts into our target demo for *Raw* and *SmackDown!*" Hunter wasn't
sure if Vince was making a joke, but he laughed anyway. He wasn't the only one.

"This is Batista's first mission," Vince said, sounding like a proud papa. "He just came off his six-week
training rotation in Washington."

"How's that torn tricep doing?" Chavo asked with
a laugh.

"I thought I saw him dancing out in that club down
in Philly last week," Cena joked.

Hunter allowed himself a smile. Fake injuries
were the perfect cover to send the Superstars down to
Virginia for NSA training. With over a dozen actual
wrestling injuries per year plaguing the WWE, it
didn't look too suspicious when a wrestler disap-
peared for "rehab." At this very moment Booker T,
Benoit, Parisi, and Stone Cold were all out on med-

ical. That's also why it was so hard to know which of the wrestlers had been approached to work for the NSA. Hunter knew that NSA operatives still numbered less than half of the WWE roster, but that number was growing every other month. As far as he knew, no two wrestlers went through training at the same time. Until now, he wasn't even aware that anyone had even worked together. For some reason, the NSA preferred to keep them all separate.

"Here's the problem," Vince said, lowering his voice. "The NSA is frustratingly slow at realizing just how valuable the WWE has been so far. This is our time to prove to them that we're not just errand boys. Do me proud." Vince stood tall and brought his volume back to normal as Phil Thompson returned to the room, carrying a laptop. "And don't forget. We've got a press event at the Garden Saturday at nine in the morning," Vince added.

"Nine o'clock," Cena mock-whined. "What self-respecting wrestler gets up before noon?"

"Followed by prep for the weekend matches leading up to *Raw,*" Vince continued. "Which Batista will be joining us on this week. Which is just my way of saying you've all got public commitments that need to be kept. Whatever you do, this mission has to be complete by the weekend. I can't have five of my Superstars failing to show up and people asking questions."

"You seem pretty sure that I've got clearance to assign them the mission," Thompson said.

"I am."

Thompson shook his head in resignation as he put the laptop down on the gym's juice bar. He ran a cable from the computer to a TV sitting on a pedestal beside him and hit a button on the keyboard. A moment later, Hunter saw a familiar face on the screen.

"Garrett Fischer," Thompson said, introducing the rest of the team to the man Hunter had met earlier. "Small-time hood that recently started making impressive inroads in the meth trade. He's taken his show on the road, distributing the highest-grade meth produced in the U.S. and shipping it all over the country. And when I say high quality, I mean he isn't knocking over drugstores to take their cough syrup supply. We think he's importing the chemicals through a series of shell companies. Hunter was tasked with making contact with Fischer to find out how he was getting chemicals into the country."

Thompson pressed a key on the computer, and a picture of Trent Gorman came up onscreen. "Fischer's money guy. We flipped him to our side when it became clear that Fischer was becoming a bigger fish. Trent's a nervous guy who doesn't seem as ready for the big time as his boss. He got Hunter into the organization this morning, since we didn't trust Trent to be strong enough to be a mole on his own."

"But that's not the reason I've brought you all in," Vince interrupted. "Hunter would have been fine with this one on his own. But Phil here saw something in video Hunter obtained this morning that caused him . . . some concern."

"Yes, Vince," Thompson said without a glance in Vince's direction. He hit another key on the laptop, and the screen showed an image of the man from this morning. It wasn't from the video Hunter had obtained, though. This was a nice three-quarter color photo of the man in an even nicer suit than the one he had on this morning. This wasn't a mug shot or anything. Far from it. Hunter had been in the business long enough to know a publicity photo when he saw one.

"Dietrich Masterson," Thompson said. "Imagine if the Mafia was in charge of a Fortune 500 company."

"They aren't?" Cena asked.

Thompson ignored the comment. "Masterson would be the CEO and godfather all wrapped up in one. He has his hand in dozens of illegal operations, from simple drug running to weapons transporting to high-tech fraud. He's been under surveillance for years, and we have video—like Hunter's—of him meeting with a wide variety of criminals."

"So why haven't you brought him in?" Torrie asked.

"It's not a crime to keep company with bad people," Thompson said. "What we lack is proof that he's doing business with any of them. As Hunter will tell you, he had to go through some pretty formidable security just to visit a meth lab today."

Everyone looked at Hunter. He just nodded his head in agreement.

"Masterson is paranoid about security," Thompson said.

"Gee, man," Chavo interrupted. "Is it really paranoia? I mean, seems to me he's got some people after him."

"Which is where you all come in," Thompson said. "As you all know, I'm opposed to this mission. I don't think you have the proper training to deal with someone at Masterson's level."

"Thanks for the vote of confidence," Batista said.

Thompson looked directly in the wrestler's eyes, asserting his own position of power against a man who would have towered over him had Batista been standing. "The vote of confidence is, I'm letting you take this mission. I really wouldn't expect anything more from me if I were you."

Vince cleared his throat. "The mission?"

"Find evidence to link Masterson to Fischer's operation," Phil said.

"Seems to me like we got that on tape," Hunter said.

"*Actual* evidence," Phil said. "Proof. Paper trail. Computer files. Anything that can be used in a court of law. We've already tried phone taps, email intercepts, and high-powered listening devices on Masterson. We've got nothing. Now it's time for you to see what you can do." Hunter didn't mistake the petulant challenge in Thompson's tone.

"You're really gonna let us have at him?" Hunter asked. "Just like that? You're not afraid of us messing up any ongoing investigations?"

"Of course I am," Thompson said. "But the convenient thing about Masterson is, he's got a lot of enemies. Who's to say you're not one of them? You want to play with the big boys, fine. You're going to learn just how black ops your team is."

"This the speech about us getting caught or captured?" Chavo asked.

"This is that speech," Vince confirmed before Thompson could answer for himself. "We're on our own on this one. The government boys won't be pulling our asses out of the fire when things get too hot. This is purely a volunteer mission. I leave it to each of you to decide for yourselves whether or not you want to do it."

John Cena was the quickest to respond. "Seems to me this is exactly the kind of thing we all signed up for."

"About time we got down to business," Hunter added.

chapter
five

"That's so *hot!*" the pair of blond party girls yelled
out as they stumbled drunkenly out of the restaurant
with their dresses askew and their high-priced shoes
dangling from their hands. The crowd of people
jostling for position at the door looked very much
like the scene the minute the doors opened to let in
the crowd for *WrestleMania.* There was even a line of
paparazzi jockeying for position behind a velvet rope,
hoping for a star sighting or two.

Torrie flipped her long brown-wigged hair in front
of her face and leaned into John Cena so they both
blocked each other from any stray photos. It wasn't

like these A-list celebrity stalkers would probably
recognize a Superstar wrestler even dressed in a ring
outfit, but Torrie didn't want to risk it. One shot
of Torrie Wilson and John Cena out on the town
together would set certain chat rooms abuzz with
gossip. Mind you, none of those chat rooms were
probably on the sites for *Star* or *Us Weekly.* Using
Cena's considerable presence, the two pushed their
way through the crowd and into the doorway.

Magma had been open for less than a month, and
it was already the talk of Manhattan. Over a dozen
local magazines and newspapers had showed their
lack of originality, all calling Magma the hot new
eatery for those with discriminating palates and
strong stomachs. The gimmick of Magma was all in
the spices, as the celebrity chef boasted the hottest
menu this side of the Mason-Dixon.

The restaurant was hardly Torrie Wilson's style.
It wasn't the menu that was the issue, it was the patrons. Once they got inside, the waiting room was
full of arrogant and pretentious people, each clearly
acting like they were more important than the next.
She could tell this without any one of them having
to open their mouths. Unfortunately, most of them
weren't exactly being quiet. Each pompous ass felt
that he or she should be seated immediately, no matter what the order of arrival. This was going to make

her and John's job all the more difficult. Luckily, she knew that John was more than up to the challenge.

" 'Scuse me," John said as he pushed past a woman boasting so many face-lifts that Torrie was surprised the woman's eyes weren't on the top of her head. "Reservation for two," he told the hostess. "Name's Charleston."

Torrie wasn't sure if he had come up with the name because of the dance or the candy bar, but it certainly fit in with the rest of the people around them. Of course, John Cena didn't look like any "Charleston" Torrie had ever imagined.

"I'm sorry," the hostess said, not sounding sorry in the least. "I don't seem to have you on the reservation list."

"What's that supposed to mean?" John asked in a voice considerably above polite conversation.

The hostess blinked twice, but remained calm. Even though the restaurant hadn't been open long, Torrie suspected that the woman had been through this kind of thing before. "When did you make the reservation, sir?"

"I don't know," John said in the most condescending manner possible, like it was the hostess's fault. "My secretary made it. For tonight. Eight o'clock. Look again. Thomas Charleston."

The hostess went down the list again even though she, Torrie, John, and everyone within earshot knew she was not going to find anything. "I'm sorry, sir, but there is no record of your reservation."

John looked at Torrie with the kind of anger traditionally held for inside the ring. "You wanted to come here, not me. You deal with this bitch."

"Thomas!" Torrie squealed as if she was shocked by his behavior.

"Sir," the hostess said coolly. Torrie gave the woman credit, she was standing tall and not about to back down now. "I am going to have to ask you to leave."

"The hell I'm leaving. We have a reservation. Eight o'clock. Sound familiar?" John raged, getting the attention of *everyone* in the waiting area and half the restaurant as well. Torrie just hoped none of the photographers outside caught wind of what was going on. "Pro Wrestler Goes to Expensive Restaurant" wasn't a story, but "Pro Wrestler Makes a Scene at Expensive Restaurant" most definitely was worth some attention.

"Darla, is there a problem here?" a well-dressed man asked as he stepped up to the hostess stand. Torrie recognized him immediately, but noted to herself that he looked far better in person than he had in his photo earlier. Dietrich Masterson was an incredibly attractive man, considering that he was a low-life criminal.

"Yeah, there's a problem here," John said. "You the manager?"

"Actually, I'm the owner," Masterson replied. "How may I help you?"

"Oh, the *owner*," John mocked to Torrie. "Isn't that nice? *You* deal with him."

Torrie rolled her eyes in the direction of the restaurant owner and leaned into the hostess stand, allowing her cleavage to help smooth over the situation. Her form-fitting red dress clung to every curve of her body in the elegant way only an expensive dress could. She was far more covered up than she ever was in the ring, but the hungry stares she was getting told her she looked sexier than she had ever before . . . even when she had been wrestling in her schoolgirl outfit. "I'm sorry, but—"

"Don't you apologize to him!" Cena shouted.

"Our reservation seems to have gotten misplaced," Torrie lied. "Is there any way you could help us out?"

The man conferred with the hostess for a moment. Torrie worried that he would actually let them into the restaurant. That was the problem with places like this; sometimes they'd let anybody in to avoid a scene as opposed to just kicking them out on their asses, where they—John, at least—belonged at the moment.

"Miss," Masterson said, "we may be able to find something for you and your husband, if you . . . "

"Husband?!" John barked. "You think this bitch has managed to get her claws in me yet? No fucking way."

Torrie had to give Masterson credit. He visibly stiffened on hearing the word *bitch*. Torrie almost missed the barely perceptible nod of his head, but she couldn't help but notice when the two burly bouncers came up on either side of John. She didn't think they worked for the restaurant, though, because they looked exactly like the two guys that Hunter had described seeing at the warehouse with Masterson earlier.

"Excuse me, sir. If you'll come with us," one of the men said.

"And who the hell are you?" John asked. "Tweedledum and Tweedledumber? Get your hands off me!"

There wasn't a doubt in Torrie's mind that John Cena could take on both of the bouncers, and half the restaurant staff, for that matter. But Thomas Charleston was the kind of guy that was all bark and no bite. Sure, he screamed and hollered as he was forced out of the restaurant, but he didn't give the bouncers the asskicking Torrie knew he could. She knew that part was killing John.

Once he was outside and things had calmed down, Torrie turned her attention back to the restaurant owner. "I'm so sorry about him," Torrie said. "If it's any consolation, I was planning on dumping him after he took me to dinner here. I just figured I'd never be able to get a reservation on my own. Who knew his name would be useless as well."

"As I was about to say," the owner replied. Torrie wasn't sure if he was leaning closely to her and speaking softly because he didn't want any of the other patrons to hear, or for some other reason. She hoped for the latter. It would make her job easier. "I think something can be arranged. If you do still wish to dine here, I know my table is still open. I would be happy to give it up for someone as lovely as yourself."

"Oh, I couldn't let you do that," Torrie said.

"Not a problem at all."

"But"—Torrie threw on a pout—"to eat here alone? With everyone staring at me, after that scene? I don't know."

"Well," the owner said, "I was just having drinks with some friends. I could be convinced to join you."

"Would you? Please?"

"Certainly," he said as he grabbed a menu from the hostess. "Right this way." He led her through the black curtain into the dining area. Sparkling

white tablecloths and shiny silver chairs comple-
mented the austere look of the blond wood floors.
They weaved their way through the tables to a
booth along the back wall. *The perfect table to sur-
vey the restaurant from,* she noted. Masterson allowed Torrie to slide in on the end. "And if I could
ask the name of my dinner companion for the
evening?"

Torrie lifted her hand and provided him with her
cover. "Larkin. Larkin Malloy."

"Dietrich Masterson," he said, taking her hand and
giving it a gentle kiss. "It is enchanting to meet you.
Now, if you'll pardon me for just one moment."

"Certainly," Torrie said. She watched him cross
the dining room, greeting various patrons as he
passed on the way to the bar, where two equally well
dressed businessmen were seated at a small table. If
Torrie wasn't mistaken—and she wasn't—the men
were local politicians of some prominence. Masterson spoke with them briefly, probably apologizing
for the fact that he was about to blow them off. The
men looked annoyed, but when Masterson directed
their attention to his table, their expressions changed
to more understanding. Suddenly finding herself the
center of attention, Torrie gave a slight wave. The
grinning fools waved back.

Dietrich returned quickly, sliding into the other

side of the booth. Their waiter was immediately on them. Torrie couldn't blame the guy. He knew it was his job to keep the boss happy. Torrie didn't even bother to open her menu, trusting the restaurateur to know the best items in the place. Masterson ordered a jambalaya for Torrie (or "Larkin"), and some kind of spicy chicken dish for himself. Torrie couldn't even begin to pronounce the name. She also allowed him to pick the wine, even though she was a Cosmo girl herself. While they waited for their meal, she filled him in on Larkin's life story, having spent the better part of the afternoon developing it just for him. Vince had told her that men with as many secrets as Masterson seldom offer up anything about themselves in the early part of a relationship. Not that she needed anyone to tell her that particular piece of information. Men with *no* secrets behaved that way as well. But Torrie had listened respectfully to the chairman at the time, fully knowing that the one area of undercover work she didn't need any assistance with was the part that pertained to men.

By the time the meal arrived, Torrie knew Masterson believed "Larkin's" fictional life as the daughter of a banker bored with the jet-set lifestyle and looking for something more meaningful to spend her time on. The conversation had been broken up by several phone calls Masterson took on his cell. Each time, Torrie politely feigned lack of interest as she listened to every word he said. She could understand how the NSA signal intercepts netted nothing worthwhile when they eavesdropped on his calls. Masterson masterfully weaved his way through conversations in generalities and couched conversation. He could have just as easily been talking about shipments of plutonium as potatoes on one of the calls.

"Sorry about that," Masterson said as he put the phone aside to take up his fork. "Unfortunately my business doesn't keep to business hours."

"That's okay," Torrie said between bites of her food. It wasn't nearly as spicy as she had anticipated. Certainly nothing compared to the meals she'd had down on their tours down South. "I imagine running a restaurant is time-consuming."

Masterson laughed politely. "Oh, no. This is just a pastime of mine. A hobby, if you will. It's not my main business."

"Oh," Torrie said. "Then what is it you do?"

"One could say that I dabble," Masterson explained. "I have my finger in a variety of enterprises. My restaurants and nightclubs are really just for show." Torrie already knew that about him. In the afternoon brief she had learned that the restaurants and clubs gave him the legitimate public face to cover for his criminal activities. They probably also provided him a way to launder his money, though nothing had yet been proven. The NSA had been unable to get in with any of his money men, like they did with that Trent guy who had brought Hunter into the meth business.

"Excuse me." Masterson apologized yet again as his phone rang for the fourth time in the meal. This conversation was longer than the others, but still resulted in no solid leads. He could have very well been talking to his mother for the amount of business that he actually conducted on the phone. Yet Torrie didn't doubt for a second that under the well wishes and talk of weekend plans, there was some code going back and forth. She doubted Masterson was the kind of person that would be so rude to take a phone call during dinner only to talk about nothing. No, he was definitely up to *something.*

The call ended, and they continued their dinner in pleasantly fake conversation. The few questions Torrie asked Masterson netted answers that she assumed were as much lies as "Larkin's" contributions. But the point of this unexpected dinner wasn't to pump him for information. That would come later. This was Torrie's chance to meet him and make a good impression. Apparently she had done just that; by the time their sorbet desserts came around, he had made sure to get her phone number.

"That is," he said, "if your boyfriend doesn't mind."

"What boyfriend?" she asked as she took a spoonful of mango-flavored sorbet and slid it between her lips.

chapter
six

The next morning, while Torrie slept in for that evening's mission, Chavo Guerrero and Batista were already on the job like thousands of other working stiffs. They even looked like working stiffs in the coveralls and tool belts. Chavo knew Batista much preferred his crisp suits, and the coverall didn't quite fit the big guy—he looked uncomfortable in it.

They drove the "borrowed" Con Edison truck through the Decatur section of Brooklyn and as close to Fischer's warehouse as they dared without risking unwanted attention. It would have been easier if they could have pulled onto the blacktop in front of the warehouse, but they needed to stay out on the street to avoid suspicion. Hunter had filled them in on the external cameras, so they knew they had to remain in the truck so they wouldn't be seen either. It wouldn't be long before people inside the building noticed their truck. They would have to act quickly.

"Setting up the connection," Chavo said from the back of the truck as Batista pulled the emergency brake.

"Need help?" Batista asked.

"I got it," Chavo said. "Just keep the engine running." He didn't like having to be teamed with Batista on this one. Not that he didn't like the guy— Batista had said wonderful things about Chavo's uncle Eddie Guerrero at his memorial. But this was Batista's first mission, and Chavo was still pretty new to fieldwork himself. He didn't need the additional stress of having someone looking to him for direction.

Chavo shook that pointless concern out of his mind as his fingers ran over the keyboard while the computer tried to make a connection. Hunter had mentioned that Fischer's computers were on a wireless system. To Chavo, that seemed an unnecessary risk, but one that would hopefully give them an in. Since Hunter couldn't risk bringing any outside equipment into the warehouse, this was their best bet to get information off Fischer's server. Even though the guy wasn't exactly an impressive target, Fischer was overseeing a cross-country drug operation. Considering he had no files in his office, it all had to be on the computer. The snitch, Trent Gorman, had told the NSA as much. If Chavo could tap into the computer through the wireless connection, he could pull the files and get out of there. The only problem was, the terminal was not making the connection.

Chavo had suspected it wouldn't be this easy. The NSA computers were some of the most powerful technology Chavo had ever seen, but they couldn't make contact with something that wasn't there. With Dietrich Masterson in the mix, Thompson warned, security would be tight. The walls had obviously been reinforced to block any outside attempts at connecting with the wireless system. That meant only one other option.

"Time to pull out," Chavo said as he moved to the front of the truck. "We're on to Plan B."

"Plan B?" Batista asked as he released the emergency brake.

"Just follow my lead," Chavo said as they pulled out onto the street. He gave Batista the directions that he had memorized before they headed out. The route had them turning through the maze of streets for several blocks until they reached their destination.

Chavo instructed Batista to park once they were about ten blocks from the warehouse. This area surrounding the industrial area was residential, so the sight of Con Ed guys strolling around or lowering themselves down manholes wouldn't even earn a second look.

"How the hell did we get picked for this job? What do I know about computers?" Batista asked as Chavo pulled equipment out of the truck and handed it to him. Chavo thought if Batista was annoyed now, there was no telling how he'd react in a few minutes. Plan B was supposed to remain a secret from Batista until the last possible moment. The big guy was on the team for so many reasons—his incomprehensible strength, his ability to intimidate the enemy with a simple look, his hand-to-hand combat skill, and on and on. The Animal was fearless . . . except for one little-known problem: he hated small spaces. Vince saw this task as a way to start Batista on the road to beating his lone fear. Too bad for Chavo that he was the one that had to be in charge of taking Batista down that road.

Chavo threw the equipment bag over his shoulder, shut the truck doors, and took the orange three-piece screen from Batista. He walked a couple steps over to the manhole cover and set the orange screen around it, then braced for impact.

"What's that for?" Batista asked. Chavo didn't bother to answer. He knew the answer would come soon enough. And from the look on his partner's face, Chavo could tell it was now.

"Aw, *hell* no," Batista said, loudly enough to scare a couple kids on their way to school.

"This is the spot where we have to go in," Chavo said, pointing down to the sewer cover. "The walls of the warehouse are blocking the signal. Thompson thinks there's a chance we can connect *under* the building. You got all that in the briefing with Vince and Phil, didn't you?"

"Right. Funny. Let's get back in the truck."

"I'm not being funny," Chavo said. "I thought you knew."

"I wasn't told nothing about this."

"You got to be kidding me! When they told me the plan, the first thing I said was, 'You told Batista this?' and they said, 'Oh, yeah, we just talked to him.' So I said, 'And he's okay with the conduit thing?' and they said, 'He's excited about the plan. He can't wait to kick some ass.' I think to myself, 'Ass-kicking, that sounds like Batista, I guess they did talk to him.' But then I said, 'You know he doesn't like small spaces, right?' And they said, 'No, he never mentioned it. He was too geared up.' So I bought it. Man, I can't believe this! They lied to me." Chavo hoped his fast talking and false hostility were enough to keep Batista thinking this was the right story.

"They told you this?" Batista asked.

"Man, they played us both," Chavo said. "But now we're here, we can't not go down. I mean, Hunter's counting on us, man. We can't leave him hanging." Chavo knew it was risky to mention of Hunter here. Hunter hadn't proven to be the most reliable associate Batista had in the past. Still, their old membership together in Evolution *had* to carry some weight with Batista, especially considering how they were all working for a larger goal at the moment.

Batista towered over the manhole cover for a good minute. He seemed to be weighing his options: either go down or go back and report a failure. While Chavo knew neither option was all that appealing, there was only one way to go as far as he was concerned. He figured Batista would eventually come up with it on his own, but it wouldn't hurt to help it along. "I need you down there with me, man. In case they anticipated the weakness and have security under the building. I can't hack into the system *and* watch my back at the same time."

"Damn," Batista said softly.

"So you're going to go in?"

"You think I'm going to head back to HQ, look

that Thompson twink in the eye, and tell him I couldn't complete this mission?"

As far as Chavo was concerned, that must have been why Phil Thompson knew the WWE Superstars would be a great addition to his agency; they refused to admit defeat.

Chavo pried the manhole cover off and they stared down into it. The light from the street didn't give them enough visibility to see past the first three rungs of the built-in ladder. There was just darkness after that.

"You first," Chavo said.

"No fucking way."

"I'm kidding," Chavo said. "Follow me." Chavo turned around and dropped his right foot onto the ladder. He looked up at his partner. He had seen Batista face down some of the meanest competitors in the ring. Triple H. Mark Henry. They were nothing to this man. Yet here he was frightened by a little hole in the ground. Chavo wasn't making light of the situation. He knew about fear. He had overcome it himself many times over the years, both in the ring and out. But right now there was a job that needed to be done. And the only thing Chavo could think about was the job. Well, that and the fact that he was really glad he wasn't Batista at that moment.

• • •

Talk about the gates of hell, Batista thought to himself.

He watched as the darkness swallowed Chavo. Darkness wasn't the problem, though. The tight confines and lack of air were what bothered him the most. It wasn't natural for a six-and-a-half-foot-tall, three-hundred-and-some-odd-pound man to be climbing down into the sewers. He wasn't Buffy the freakin' Vampire Slayer. He preferred his enemies aboveground. At the same time, he knew he couldn't let his partner go in unprotected.

"I'm down," Chavo called up from the dark hole. "Batista?"

"I'm comin'," Batista growled as he set his left foot on the top rung. *Just think you're climbing into the ring,* he tried to tell himself. The only problem with that was, you had to climb *up* into the ring, not *down* into the depths below. The other problem was, the ring was about twenty by twenty feet, whereas a manhole was . . . considerably smaller. Batista was able to get the lower half of his body into the hole with no problem, but as more and more of his bulk moved down the ladder, he could feel the world closing in on him. He had to stop before his upper torso had crossed below street level. This would be the last of the fresh air and sky for a while. He wasn't exactly in a hurry to leave it.

"You okay, man?" asked Chavo's muffled voice from below.

Batista didn't answer. He took several deep breaths and continued the descent. The metal ring surrounding the hole pressed against his shoulders as he squeezed down, causing a minor panic attack. Batista told himself, *Keep moving . . . keep moving,* until the words became a mantra with each additional rung. Finally he felt concrete beneath his shoes as his feet were firmly on the ground. His eyes had not left the top of the manhole and the patch of light blue he could see through it.

"Need a minute?" Chavo asked as he handed Batista the flashlight.

"Yeah," Batista grunted as he tore his eyes off the exit and looked out at the tunnel ahead of him. He refused to move one step until his eyes adjusted to the dim light. It was one thing to plunge ahead through a closed and cramped space, it was another entirely to do it blindly.

Chavo was looking down at his handheld GPS system. Hoping for something else to focus on beyond the walls that seemed to be closing in on him, Batista stole a glance over Chavo's shoulder. The screen showed a map of the underground tunnels, with a red line that led right under the warehouse where Fischer's operation was housed. Batista took some solace in the fact that they wouldn't get trapped belowground as long as they had that map with them. Of course, that only led him to start imagining all the ways they could lose the map. Never before had he had so much relying on a pair of double-A batteries.

"Ready to move?" Chavo asked, looking up from the screen.

"No," Batista said. "But let's go."

Chavo gave him a reassuring smile as he started on his way down the underground labyrinth. Batista had no choice but to follow. He was forced to walk with a slight hunch, as the ceiling was not built to his height specifications. Luckily the walls were spaced out so that two average-sized men could walk side by side. Two averaged-sized wrestlers were able to walk one behind another, with some space between their bodies and the walls. For not the first time in his life Batista cursed his size, wishing he had more of a cruiserweight build like Chavo. Sure, others cowered under Batista in the ring, but he now felt just like he did the time someone tried to put him in a Mini Cooper.

Batista focused his thoughts on the small amount of extra space between him and the walls while trying to ignore the fact that his head would smack into the ceiling if he stood upright. While his thoughts were focused on *all* the nonexistent extra space around him, his eyes were locked on his feet. So long as he kept reminding himself to put one foot in front of the other, he didn't have to think about the fact that the ceiling seemed to be getting lower, and the walls closer.

At first Batista thought it was all in his mind. His fear was just messing with his head; the tunnel wasn't getting any smaller. But he could only convince himself of that for so long. After three turns down the path as he followed Chavo, Batista could feel his arms brushing against the walls. He knew that he was walking in a much lower crouch than he had started with. He couldn't lie to himself anymore: the tunnel was getting smaller. Not only that, but he was going down a slight hill as well. They were getting deeper and deeper into the darkness. The small flashlight he was carrying wasn't doing much to relieve the tension. In fact, all it was really doing was reminding him of the concrete tomb around him.

Still, Batista focused on his feet and ignored his own rapid breathing and the intense pounding of his heart. He wasn't sure if Chavo could hear the involuntary sounds his breath and heart were making, but his partner seemed to sense something was wrong. "We're almost there," Chavo said reassuringly. "The tunnel should be opening up more under the warehouse."

Batista couldn't even bring himself to respond. Every fiber of his being was focused on forward progression. Yet there was a constant internal battle with the parts of his mind that wanted him to turn and run back to that open manhole and the fresh air and beautiful blue sky. The little voice in the back of Batista's mind had almost convinced him to do just that when another voice slipped in. It was Chavo's. "Here we are, man. You can look up now."

Batista hadn't noticed that the walls and ceiling were no longer pressing against his body. When he finally took his eyes off his feet, he saw that he was in an underground chamber, a connecting room of some kind. Tunnels went out in different directions, all coming together at this junction. But most importantly, the room was larger than a wrestling ring and several feet taller than even Big Show. It was still dark and underground, but this he could manage much better than the cramped tunnel.

"What's that?" Batista asked as he shined his light up at the tunnel ceiling. There seemed to be a crudely cut panel above them.

"Access hatch?" Chavo whispered. "To get up to the warehouse? There's no mention of it on the map."

"So Fischer's meth lab is right above us?" Batista asked, matching Chavo's whisper. "We better hurry up and get out of here, then."

Chavo pulled the laptop computer out of his satchel. Since there was nowhere for him to put the thing except the ground, Batista held out his arms for Chavo to rest the computer on. Batista couldn't help but be a little upset that he had come all this way to be nothing more than a piece of furniture. Still, if he had let Chavo go the underground route on his own and something had happened, Batista never would have forgiven himself.

The computer came to life, and Chavo started typing in commands. "It's searching for a connection," he said. "This shouldn't take too long."

Batista replayed that comment over and over in his mind to remind himself that he had to wait only a bit longer. Once the computer made its connections, Chavo would work his technological magic and pull everything off the files from the computers above them. At least some good came from those hours of video-game playing Chavo had sat through when he should have been prepping for matches. And if Chavo managed to get them out of there quickly, Batista promised to buy the guy the new PS3 as soon as it hit the market.

"Uh-oh," Chavo said.

Batista didn't like the sound of that.

"It's not connecting," Chavo explained. "Let me see if I can try something else."

"Whatever," Batista said. "Just hurry."

Again, Batista focused on looking down as he felt the walls closing in on him. This time it was all in his mind; the chamber wasn't physically getting any smaller. But that didn't matter. If he stared too much at the walls and ceiling, he would convince himself that they were coming in on him. However, had he allowed himself to look up, he might have seen the tiny pinpoint of red light flashing in the corner.

chapter
seven

Hunter worked to set up the computer left for him in
the closet of an office he had been assigned. Hacking
wasn't his specialty, but Hunter still gave it a go to
see if he could get into Fischer's files by logging onto
the server. The system they'd set up was as impressive as the security in the building itself, especially
considering only a handful of people were actually
given access to computers.

Within a couple minutes Hunter gave up on the
computer entirely. *If only I could get one of those
NSA gadgets in here,* he thought. But sneaking in
any hacking devices would be foolhardy, considering

the extreme security setup he had just been walked through. He was lucky to get through with his video camera glasses. And he knew that only had to do with the fact that the glasses were made with experimental state-of-the-art polymers that couldn't be read by any security system known to the NSA. But since that polymer hadn't been adapted into other technology yet, he'd have to leave the hacking to an expert like Chavo was supposed to be.

Instead, Hunter focused on his abbreviated tour of the facility. What little he had learned about the illegal operation was already impressive. Security on the place was tight, with redundancy after redundancy in place in case anything failed. It would have been impossible for the NSA to get in without someone already on the inside. But now that the mission was more than just taking down a drug lab, they needed to get whatever information they could before closing down the operation.

"Sorry about that," Fischer said as he returned from the security booth. "I needed to take that call."

"Seems a bit inconvenient having to go to the security booth to do business," Hunter pointed out.

"Not my idea," Fischer said. "But it does cut down on the risk of anyone making unsupervised calls."

"I guess."

"So," Fischer said as he sat in the one guest chair that could fit in the room, "any questions?"

Hell, yeah, Hunter thought. He had a ton of questions. The problem was that he didn't know which ones would get a response. "When do we go over the benefits package?" he joked.

Fischer's face was a mask of confusion until he got the joke. He then overcompensated by laughing way more than the line required. Hunter briefly wondered if the NSA had overestimated their adversary. *Do they really need an entire team to get this guy?* But he reminded himself about the bigger fish, Dietrich Masterson, and continued to play his part.

"There any reason you didn't want to take me into the lab?" Hunter asked. That was the one part of the tour Fischer had specifically avoided. Hunter couldn't imagine why "Mike" would need to see it, but the NSA agent side of him needed a full grasp of the setup if the government organization was going to raid the place someday.

Fischer blew off the question. "You know those lab types. They get so nervous around strangers."

Hunter nodded as if he had any idea what Fischer was talking about. The word *lab* didn't mean that a meth lab was operated by geeky guys in glasses with no social lives. He knew that meth was made by people from all walks of life, from low-life drug pushers to suburban housewives—although he doubted any housewives were involved in making this particular brand of poison.

From what Hunter had learned in his mission prep, ephedrine was a major ingredient in synthesized meth-amphetamine. The average lab had to settle for extracting ephedrine from over-the-counter congestion medications because they couldn't get straight stuff. That's why people had to go to the pharmacist to get over-the-counter medicine at Target nowadays, and nobody was allowed to buy in bulk. By its very nature, this distilling process started them out with lower-quality ephedrine, which would result in a less pure synthetic meth.

Some of Fischer's stock had been found on the streets and traced back to his organization. NSA labs confirmed that the process used in producing the drug involved large quantities of metallic sodium as the catalyst for the reaction that turned ephedrine into meth. The use of sodium for this made the process easier and the product more potent. The problem was that metallic sodium was hard to obtain in the States, which meant Fischer had to be getting shipments from outside of the U.S. When border security got involved, it became an issue too big for the NSA normally to hand off to the DEA.

The other problem with this method of production

was that it created an extremely toxic byproduct. Twelve pounds of toxic waste were collected in barrels for every pound of the drug cooked up. Hunter had seen a huge collection of barrels in the annex building during his tour, but Fischer didn't bother to point out what they were. Not that Hunter couldn't figure it out on his own. The barrels contained something the new upscale residents of Brooklyn wouldn't want in their backyard.

"So, what's the first order of business?" Hunter asked as he leaned on his desk.

"We've got a move coming Friday," Fischer said. "Out with the old, in with the new, so to speak."

"How so?"

"I'm sure you know that meth production results in some rather unfortunate byproducts."

"Nice way to refer to toxic waste."

"Call it what you want." Fischer shrugged. "It's not something we like to keep around for too long." Hunter nodded. It was the first logical thing Fischer had said since they met. "So when we bring in the new batch of chemicals, we also ship out the byproducts," Fischer continued. "All done under the cover of nightfall."

"Because nobody would notice a bunch of trucks offloading in the middle of the night?" Hunter asked. It seemed much smarter to him to do it during normal business hours, when they'd attract less attention.

"Timing isn't the issue on this end," Fischer said. "It's where we're getting the chemicals from and where the waste is going to. That's where the whole cover-of-nightfall crap works for us."

"So where *are* we getting the chemicals from, and where is the waste going to go?"

"The chemicals are at the Port of Newark," Fischer said.

Hunter raised an eyebrow. "How'd you manage to get that past customs?"

"It isn't that hard, considering only a handful of containers are checked on every ship that comes in," Fischer said. "From there it's just a matter of getting the containers out without anyone noticing where they're going."

"And it helps to do that at night to avoid the paperwork," Hunter reasoned.

"Exactly," Fischer said. "You cut through too much red tape, and people start asking questions. But a few containers disappear, and the exact opposite happens. People start covering things up so they don't get in trouble. It's a nice way to have other people do the work for you, don't you think?"

Hunter smiled through the disgust he felt for this man. He couldn't wait to send Fischer to prison for a long time. Not just because the guy was involved in illegal activities, but because the asshole was so damned smug about it.

"And where is the toxic stuff going?" Hunter asked. Even though the port information was the goal of his mission, the NSA would clearly find a toxic dumping ground to be fairly important too.

"All in good time," Fischer said.

Hunter didn't want to press too much during "Mike's" trial period. Still, he did have a job to do. "Good time?" Hunter joked. "Today's my first day, and you want this all ready by tomorrow night?"

"Trent said you were the best."

"That I am," Hunter said. "You got enough guys for a move like this?"

"That's why you're here," Fischer said. "Trent's going to handle the business end. I need someone to keep an eye on the men. Could use some extra guys too. Trent says you got connections. To find guys that don't ask questions?"

Hunter gave a nod.

"Good," Fischer said. "Most of the guys we'll just need to load the trucks at the port tomorrow night. But we could use a couple on this end as well. Any chance you could get a pair of guys here this afternoon? I'd like to get them acquainted with the operation as soon as possible."

"Don't see why that would be a problem," Hunter said. Actually, he *knew* it wouldn't be a problem, considering the guys he had in mind were quite close at the moment.

A tap on the doorframe brought a halt to the conversation. Hunter looked up to see the same black guy who had run them through security the day earlier. The guy was so large he had to enter the room slightly sideways. Between him and Hunter, there was hardly room for air in the small office.

"We got a problem," the guy said. "The intruder alarm is going off at the back door."

Hunter didn't like the sound of that. It was possible that Fischer was about to meet his two new employees a little sooner than anyone anticipated.

chapter
eight

Hunter took in the situation. Fischer didn't seem all that bothered by the alarm. In fact, he didn't seem to care at all. "Ray," Fischer said to the guy in the doorway, "I want you to meet Mike. He'll be helping out around here, keeping the guys in line."

Hunter stood and shook hands with Ray. The two men matched grips as they shook, each trying to show dominance with a simple greeting. He had seen the guy hovering around during his tour of the place earlier, as well as when Hunter entered the warehouse. Still, they hadn't been formally introduced until now. From the way the workers gave Ray his space, it was clear that he wasn't just another lackey.

"Ray's head of security here," Fischer said. "Hell, he *is* security here."

"We've got a red light by the back door," Ray insisted.

"Probably just another rat," Fischer said with a dismissive wave. "Damn things have been tripping the alarm since we put it in."

"Still, I'm gonna check it out," Ray said.

"Back door?" Hunter asked. He hadn't seen any back door when Fischer took him on his walk-through. He hadn't seen any doors at all except the security entrance and the loading bay door.

"It's nothing to worry about," Fischer said. But Hunter could see a flash of annoyance in Fischer's eyes. More importantly, Hunter noticed that Ray seemed to be sizing him up to see how "Mike" played off Fischer's reactions.

"Still," Hunter said, "if you want me to coordinate your operations here, I'm going to need to know about things like back doors and security. Unless you don't think you can trust me. Then we've got bigger problems."

"That's not it at all, Mike," Fischer said.

"Good," Hunter said as he stood. "Then, Ray, why don't you show me this back door. We can check out the alarm together."

Ray threw a glance in Fischer's direction, but didn't bother to wait for him to respond before turning and walking out of the office. "This way," he said.

Hunter left his office with Fischer still in the guest chair. This alarm situation worried Hunter. If he was right, Chavo and Batista were digging around outside, trying to get some connection to the wireless system Fischer ran his computers off. *They wouldn't be dumb enough to get so close to the building that they'd trigger an alarm, would they?*

"You don't mind me tagging along, do you?" Hunter asked.

"Don't bother me at all," Ray said. "Fischer's the one who got his panties in a bunch. He don't like anyone knowing about his little secret."

"That didn't stop you from mentioning it in front of the new guy," Hunter pointed out.

"Helps keep the boss in line," Ray said, not even bothering to lower his voice as they walked through the warehouse. "You might not have noticed it yet, but Fischer can get kind of full of himself. I like to knock him down a peg or two from time to time. Remind him how much he needs me around here."

"And how much does he need you?" Hunter asked.

"More than he knows," Ray said confidently as he opened the door to the lab. Hunter was surprised by this development. He hadn't expected to go through the lab. This was a nice turn of events.

A smell slightly like cat piss greeted them through the open door. Hunter was glad to be getting his first look at the workroom and adjusted his eyeglasses accordingly to record every second. Fischer had pointedly left this area off the earlier tour. It was like the guy was playing games to keep Hunter from having an idea of the full scope of the operation. Hunter could understand that from a security perspective. Too bad it also destroyed any relationship Fischer had with his workers. With this kind of illegal operation, keeping people out of the loop was a surefire way to encourage them to stab him in the back. Hunter suspected that was the real reason Ray was taking him on this tour through the lab. The circuitous route they were taking seemed to parallel the storage area of the warehouse. It didn't seem like they needed to come in here at all, but Hunter was glad they had.

The operation continued to look far more professional than anyone would assume from the outside appearance of the warehouse. Sparkling clean tables, polished floors, and cutting-edge equipment filled the room. The machinery was all first-rate, though much of it was starting to rust, which was to be expected with meth production.

A dozen men and women dressed in crisp white coveralls went about their business without a word. They didn't even look up to see the new guy walking through the room. Considering that meth could just as easily be made in the bathroom of some run-down dump in the ghetto, this setup seemed like overkill to Hunter. But that's exactly why the NSA must have been interested in Fischer in the first place. It was like he was taking meth into mass production. With this kind of operation and the quality of meth Fischer was supplying, the drug would easily find its way into the better homes and businesses across the country.

Once again Hunter couldn't help but think that this operation was a bit out of Fischer's league. *This Masterson guy is clearly in deep.*

Ray led Hunter out a second door and into a back part of the warehouse. This confirmed Hunter's earlier suspicion. There was no need to take him through the lab at all. He had been in this area earlier, and they had gone around the lab to get there. If Ray was so annoyed with his boss that he would play games like these, he could definitely come in handy later.

"Where's this back door?" Hunter asked as he continued to follow Ray. "I didn't see one earlier on the tour." He also hadn't seen one on the building schematics when he prepped for the mission. Sure, there had been one when the warehouse was originally built. It wouldn't make any sense for such a large structure to have only one door and one loading dock and no other way out. But the layout indicated that the warehouse had been extended a few years back, replacing the back wall with a solid structure. The other exterior door had been turned into a throughway to get to the newer annex building. He was pretty sure these little "improvements" to the design hadn't been run past any fire marshal.

"That was only the nickel tour Fischer took you on," Ray said. "With me you get the full dollar."

Hunter was starting to like Ray. He didn't seem as full of himself as Fischer or as nervous as Trent. If he hadn't been so deep in a criminal operation, Hunter could see them being work out buds.

"Here we are," Ray said as he stopped in the center of the back room. This was the place where old equipment went to die—an oversized junk closet, Hunter had thought earlier. The room was piled with broken or rusted-out equipment, thrown haphazardly into piles because it wasn't safe to use anymore. But, as earlier, Hunter didn't see any door.

Ray enjoyed the confused look on Hunter's face for a moment. "This way," he said, nodding toward a side corner.

The men walked over to the corner, but Hunter

couldn't even see a seam in the wall that could be a hidden door. When Ray lifted a small table and moved it out of the way, Hunter realized he had been looking in the wrong place. A small square outline sat in the floor below him. As Ray gently put the table down in an out-of-the-way spot, Hunter positioned himself between Ray and the trap door.

"You really think it's a rat?" Hunter asked.

"Probably," Ray said. "Damn vermin are always setting off the alarm. Got to check it, though. Even though Fischer don't think so. 'Cause one of these days it ain't gonna be a rat."

"You sound pretty sure of that," Hunter said.

"I've been doing this kind of crap long enough to know that an operation like this, run by a guy like Fischer . . . it's eventually gonna blow up in his face. The trick is to know when it's time to get the hell out before it does."

Hunter nodded knowingly, then bent down to the trapdoor. He slid his finger into the small metal ring and lifted it slightly. "You got a gun in case?" he asked, hoping to give Chavo and Batista both a warning and time to get the hell out if they were the ones setting off the alarm. When Ray didn't answer, Hunter turned to see a gun already aimed in his direction.

"Good," Hunter said as he slowly raised the door.

This was the one flaw in the NSA's plan. Superstars were always sent in unarmed because of their high-profile nature. There were so many times Hunter had been startled by fans on the street, running up and grabbing him to say hello. The last thing he needed was for a gun to drop out of his jacket during an impromptu autograph signing. The press would be on top of him about it, dubbing him the "Armed Wrestler" or some shit like that. To avoid the issue, the NSA gave him some geeky little keychain stun gun device that looked like it couldn't take down a field mouse, much less a New York City rat, if that is what actually turned out to be in the hole.

Hunter felt a tap on his back. For a brief moment he wondered if it was the muzzle of the gun. But when he turned, he saw that it was only a flashlight.

"Where'd that come from?" Hunter asked, more loudly than the question required, considering Ray was right behind him. Ray nodded toward a shelf to his right. Hunter saved that information for later, thinking it might be necessary.

He nodded his thanks and took the light, pressing it on and shining the beam down into the tunnel. A quick scan revealed Chavo and Batista hunched in a corner, ready to pounce. They both looked much calmer now that they saw it was Hunter above them, but they also stayed in their ready positions.

Chavo held his laptop into the light and shook his head violently. Hunter took that to mean they couldn't access the wireless system from that position. If they couldn't get into the computer, they wouldn't be able to pull down all the information on the organization. Sure, they had enough evidence of the meth lab itself to put Fischer away for a while, but they needed all the facts—especially the ones that linked Fischer to Masterson. There was no doubt in Hunter's mind that the computers in the warehouse had a failsafe. One command would probably wipe the entire system the moment the NSA, DEA, or whoever came knocking at the door.

"I don't see nothin'," Hunter said to Ray. "But maybe I should go down and check it out."

"That's okay," Ray said. "Don't need you getting rabies from some rat or something."

Hunter looked down at his teammates. Even if he did insist on going down into the tunnel, Ray would stick around to keep an eye on him. Sure, Chavo could give him the tech stuff to use on the computer, but there was no way to get down and up without tipping Ray off to the fact that there were two guys down there. *That's okay,* Hunter thought. *There are ways to get around this.*

"Good point," Hunter said, keeping the door open so Chavo and Batista could listen in. "By the way, how *do* I make a phone call around here? Fischer wants me to bring in some help. Just so happens I know a couple guys in the area that could get here real fast. Faster if I don't have to leave the damn building and go back to my car to use my cell phone."

"I got the phone in my office," Ray said. "It'll just take a second."

"Well, I don't need to be *that* fast," Hunter said as he closed the trapdoor, knowing the guys got the message.

chapter
nine

Vince McMahon wasn't a fearful man by nature. True, he had been afraid from time to time over the course of his life. He knew fear. But it was never a permanent state. He felt it in brief flashes. Like when he knew he was outnumbered and outweighed in the ring. Or when his children got hurt. Or when his wrestlers did. He felt a momentary pang of fear, then it moved on to something more productive like concern, anger, or some other more useful emotion. But it never stuck around.

Until now.

Yes, Vince had felt fear like this before. He felt it

every time his Superstars went on a mission. Vince could handle anything that happened in the ring. Even the accidents were a part of the business. His people did everything in their power to make sure things were safe, but every now and then the unexpected happened. Tragedy struck. But that, to a certain degree, was also expected. NSA fieldwork was another matter entirely. No matter how many precautions the Superstars took on a mission, there was always one variable that could not be controlled: the enemy. Bitter enemies in the wrestling ring were still professionals. But the bad guys in the real world were killers—by title *and* by nature. Now Vince had five of his Superstars out there dealing with the worst of the worst. And he had *encouraged* it.

If anything happened to them, it was Vince's fault. He had gotten them into this. Sure, it was one thing to say it was for God and country, but that wasn't why they did it. They did it because Mister McMahon had asked them. Even the guys he brought into the team that hated him did it because they respected him. He tried to put that out of his mind so he would not give in to the fear. There was nothing he could do about his guys in the field. He had other things to focus on at the moment—Phil Thompson, for one.

What is that guy up to?

They had been working together for two years now. Hell, they were even in the same city Vince had been heading to when Phil approached him to join the cause. And yet in that two years Vince still didn't have a handle on the guy. He seemed like the same asshole Vince had left behind in his youth. The same scum that had forced Vince into a detour from his future. Not that Vince was complaining—following in his father's footsteps had worked out well for him. Quite well, in fact. Yet he couldn't help but wonder what would have happened if Thompson hadn't gotten in the way.

And now here he was, working for the man who had screwed him over.

No, Vince insisted. *Not for* him. *For your country.*

The ringing of the phone roused Vince from his musings. He picked it up before it could get to a second ring. "Go," he said, instead of "Hello."

"Mister McMahon, we hit a snag on the computer tap," Chavo said over the phone. "The system locked us out."

"Damn," Vince said. He didn't want to report any kind of failure back to Thompson. Luckily he wasn't due in for another hour, so this piece of information could wait.

"But we got another way in," Chavo said. "Hunter

just called us. He wants us to go undercover in the warehouse too."

"How's that gonna help us get access to the computer?" Vince asked. "Hunter said you can't get any equipment in or out of the building."

"Yeah, but he didn't know about the secret entrance when he told us that," Chavo said.

"Secret entrance?"

"Long story," Chavo said. "Look, we got everything we need in the truck to hack into the system, set up a tap into the phone, and record conversations. We just need Thompson's permission to go in. Is he there? Hunter's waiting."

"Screw Thompson," Vince said. "I'm telling you to go in. We don't want to lose this opportunity."

"Will do, Mister McMahon," Chavo said. Vince could hear the smile in his voice. Vince might not always be the most popular guy among his wrestlers, but he knew they could all get behind going around authority figures now and then.

"Be careful," Vince warned, though he didn't need to. Once they disconnected, Vince realized that contact with one of his guys hadn't eased his concern any. If anything, it had just intensified.

"You okay, Mister McMahon?" Torrie asked as she leaned in the doorway to Vince's temporary office.

"Just thinking," he replied. "Come in."

Torrie did as instructed and sat on the small couch in the office. She was dressed conservatively, which is how she usually looked when not in the ring or on a mission that required her to exploit her more visual assets. "Looks like you're having a rough morning."

"No rougher than any other," Vince said and realized with a bit of surprise that it was true. Whether in his government work or his WWE responsibilities, Vince was always under a certain amount of pressure. The thought finally made him snap out of it. Vince McMahon wasn't a whiny little baby. He was the chairman of World Wrestling Entertainment. *And it's time you started acting like it, dammit.*

"Sorry I had to call you in early," Vince said. "But I wanted to check in with you before Thompson got here. I know I don't have to tell you how important this mission is."

"No," Torrie said. "But things couldn't have gone better. Masterson and I hit it off immediately. He . . . " Torrie trailed off when they heard the sound of a cell phone ringing. It was the one that the NSA provided her. Considering that Masterson was the only person she would have given the number to, Vince didn't have to guess who was on the other line. "Speak of the devil," she said as she pulled the phone out of her purse. "Seems a little eager, if you ask me. I mean, it *is* kind of early in the day."

Vince waited for her to answer it, but she just held it in her hand. "Are you planning on getting that?" he asked.

"In a moment," she said. "Just because *he's* eager, I don't want him to think *I* am."

Vince shared a smirk with her as they waited through another ring. If there was one thing his Divas knew, it was how to attract men.

Torrie opened the phone a moment before it would have rolled over to voice mail. "Yes?" she said as Vince listened in. "Dietrich? What a wonderful surprise . . . No. It's not too early. I'm actually glad you called . . . I'd love to . . . This weekend? Well, I'm going out of town for a while. Would it seem horribly pathetic of me to suggest tonight?" Vince couldn't tell what the response was, but it elicited a boldly flirtatious laugh from Torrie. "I love it. Should I meet you there?" Vince beamed as she finished up her call, making plans with Masterson for that evening. Things were looking good. Hunter, Chavo, and Batista were in at the warehouse. Torrie was making headway with Masterson. And Cena was on call for backup should it become necessary. Things couldn't be going better—which only forced Vince to wonder, *What's next?*

chapter
ten

"These your guys?" Fischer asked as soon as Hunter walked through the security entry with Chavo and Batista. Hunter thought that was a fairly stupid question—he wasn't just going to walk into the building with random strangers.

"Yeah," he answered. "This is Chuck and Brad."

"Which is which?" Fischer asked.

"Does it matter?"

"No," Fischer said. "I guess it don't."

"Matters to me," Ray said as he handed Chavo and Batista's personal items back to them. "Look, boss, I don't mind Mike here coming in off a recommendation. But these guys are a recommendation off a rec- ommendation. Whatever happened to doing security checks around here?"

"It's okay, Ray," Hunter said. "I'll vouch for them."

"Well, now, Mike," Ray said. "You seem like an okay guy and all, but I've only known you a couple hours. I'd like a bit more background, if you don't mind."

"How 'bout a backhand?" Batista asked.

"Brad," Hunter warned.

"Ray, don't worry so much," Fischer said.

"Worrying's what you pay me for," Ray said.

"Well, you've earned your cash for the morning al- ready," Fischer said. "Take a break."

Ray gave Chavo and Batista the once-over before walking back to the security booth. Hunter could see in Ray's eyes that he was calculating just how much longer he was going to work for Fischer before mov- ing on to some other operation. Hunter wished he could do something to hurry that resignation along. It would make his life a hell of a lot easier if Ray weren't around watching him. Too bad there was no way the head of security was going to be leaving the day before an important shipment was coming in.

"So, what's the deal here?" Chavo asked. "Mike filled us in on the cargo. What do you want us to do?"

"I need someone to handle the transfer," Fischer

said. "I got some good people working for me, but they're more followers than leaders. I'm looking for a couple guys to stay here to oversee things while Mike retrieves the goods. You know, get the outgoing packages ready to load while the trucks come in to be unloaded."

"Where you gonna be?" Batista asked.

"Here," Fischer replied, as if it was the most obvious thing in the world.

Hunter shot Batista a look telling him to leave it alone. Sure, it made no sense that Fischer wouldn't prefer to keep things under control here himself. But his laziness was working for them. No need to look that proverbial gift horse in the choppers.

Thankfully, Chavo picked up on the train of thought and moved the conversation along. "Mike told us about the incoming part, but what's outgoing shipment? For some reason I think he's keeping something from us."

Chavo had already been briefed on the full operation between the parking lot and the warehouse. But he and Hunter had agreed that "Mike" probably wouldn't have filled "Chuck" in on every element. Especially considering that they would be dealing with the shipping of toxic chemicals.

"Just some byproducts of the manufacturing process," Fischer said, dismissively.

"Byproducts?" Chavo said. "Seems to me the

byproducts of a meth lab would be kind of dangerous. Like the toxic variety."

"Something like that," Fischer said with a shrug,
as if he was trying to downplay the fact that he just
admitted they'd be moving some dangerous stuff.

"What's the deal?" Batista said to Hunter. "You
bring us here to go carrying around some deadly
shit?"

"I brought you here to make some money," Hunter
said, playing "Mike" as the hard-ass. "Shouldn't matter to you if you were carrying kitties."

"Hell, seems to me kitties' claws don't cause the
same kind of trouble," Batista said. "You got hazmat
suits?"

"You *are* the hazmat suits," Fischer replied. "Don't
worry. The waste is stored in good strong containers.
We don't play games with that shit around here."

"Even so," Chavo said, "I think our prices just
doubled." Though the comment was made in a light
tone, the look on Chavo's face said, "Don't mess
with us."

Hunter waited for Fischer to make his decision. It
wasn't like the guy was going to kick them all out of
the building, but it was interesting to see the man's
mind at work. It all came down to meeting his own
needs. Hunter knew that Fischer could oversee things
in the warehouse just fine. He probably just wanted

someone else to do it for him. So far everything about this operation screamed that Fischer liked to have other people do the work for him. No wonder he hadn't gotten further before this. It was just a matter of hitching his wagon to Masterson's star. Now all Hunter had to do was find some proof of that hitch.

"Okay," Fischer said with a shrug, as if the question wasn't even worth the time he had spent thinking about it. "Mike, why don't you show the guys where the outgoing shipment is stored."

"Sure thing," Hunter said as he led Chavo and Batista off. It was impressive the way Fischer kept coming up with euphemisms for toxic waste.

As Hunter led Chavo and Batista to the warehouse annex, he saw Trent watching them from his office. Even at that distance, it was clear the guy was worried. Hunter figured he should have warned Trent that he was bringing some help in, but he hadn't had the chance to talk to him earlier. Hopefully, it wouldn't be a problem.

"So, this Ray guy, what's his problem?" Batista asked once they were out of earshot.

"Only professional in an unprofessional organization," Hunter explained.

"Which means he's gonna be on our asses, 'cause us coming in like this at the last minute is everything that's wrong with this place," Chavo guessed.

"You got it," Hunter said as they crossed into the toxic storeroom.

"Just what we need," Batista said.

"Aw, man, where's your sense of adventure?" Chavo asked. "Just makes our job more interesting."

Hunter liked Chavo's attitude. He could see them working on a team more often. It was nice to know someone had his back for a change. Though he didn't always trust Chavo in the ring, this outside work could be good.

Batista, on the other hand, was an unknown element. Sure, they had made names for themselves together in the past. But there had been a hell of a lot of water under the bridge since then. Some blood too. Hopefully none of that was going to come up on this mission.

"It should only take a dozen trips with the forklift to get everything out front," Hunter said. "There are plenty of guys around here to do the heavy lifting."

"Need to keep up our strength in case anything goes down tomorrow night," Chavo agreed.

"And want to stay as far away from this crap as possible too," Batista added.

Hunter checked to make sure they were alone, then leaned in to his two partners. "This stuff is moved last," he said. "We don't need it up front when everyone busts in to take the joint."

"Yeah," both men agreed.

"Okay," Batista said as he eyed the collection of barrels filled with toxic waste. "We've seen the stuff. Now let's get the hell out of here."

Hunter looked at Batista, then he looked at the dangerous barrels all around them. "For the first time in a long time, I'd say we're on the same page."

"Now where's this back door?" Chavo asked.

"This way," Hunter said, taking them back out of the annex. The three of them quickly moved away from the toxic storage unit. Since they already looked like a little tour group, Hunter just continued with that cover, passing the few workers who were setting up for tomorrow's move. Fischer had given most of the staff the day off in preparation for the transfer. Some guys would come back that evening to relieve the guys on hand. Then everyone would report in on Friday night for the move.

Hunter stopped the tour for a second to show Chavo and Batista the latest stock of methamphetamines. He explained how the shipments went out weekly in U-Haul trucks and other more nondescript rides at irregular intervals to keep the stuff moving. Both men were as surprised as Hunter had been by the scope of the operation. Fischer might not know entirely what he was doing, but no one could question that it seemed to be working. *For now,* Hunter thought.

Hunter continued past the stock of synthetic meth and into the back.

"This way to the break room," Hunter said loudly. Then he softly added, "Watch out for the cameras." He nodded over his shoulder toward the corner. Neither Fischer nor Ray had pointed out the security cameras on either of his two earlier tours. Not that there would have been any reason to. Still, Hunter had made sure that he knew the position of every one of them by the time Chavo and Batista got there.

Since there was no reason in the world he would be showing the two new guys the dead equipment storage room, he had to be sneaky about it. There was no doubt that Ray was watching them at the moment. Conveniently, the back storage room was right off the break room.

Hunter pulled a barely chilled soda out of the refrigerator as the guys took stock of the room. It wasn't much, but it was a dump. A board laid across two sawhorses served as a makeshift table, along with a couple of old folding chairs. There was a row of metal cots lined against the far wall for the guys to rest on during their twenty-four hour shifts. There wasn't much else beyond that. It was yet another of Fischer's failings that his office furniture was expensive and new, while his employees had nothing but crap.

"This it?" Batista asked, thinking they had come to the room with the secret exit.

"Through there," Hunter said as he opened his soda, holding it in the direction of the doorway. "The hatch is in the far right corner. There's a flashlight on the shelf beside it."

"Gotcha," Batista said.

"Cameras in there?" Chavo asked.

"Yep," Hunter said as he took a swig.

"Plan?" Chavo asked.

"Distraction," Hunter said as he checked his watch. "Give me exactly five minutes, then go."

"Will do," the guys said.

Hunter took his soda and went out to the front of the warehouse. Hopefully Ray would be alone in the security booth and wouldn't mind an interruption. If Hunter couldn't pull off this simple plan, the entire mission would be blown.

chapter
eleven

Hunter hurried back through the maze of storage shelves in the warehouse. He knew he should have given himself more than five minutes to get to Ray, but he also knew that time wasn't a luxury he possessed. If Ray was watching the new hires over the security system, he would eventually come around to check why the first thing they did when they got there was hang out in the break room. Hunter already knew that getting things past Ray was going to be the difficult part of the mission. Fischer he could handle with ease, but the security chief was another matter entirely.

As Hunter walked past the front offices, he caught movement out of the corner of his eye. Trent had hopped up from his desk and was heading straight for him. *I don't have time for this,* Hunter thought as he kept walking.

"Hey, Mike!" Trent called out, which pulled attention from a couple guys who were doing some mechanical work on the small forklift.

Hunter knew if he just ignored Trent, he'd be getting even more attention thrown his way. "What?" he asked without breaking stride. He needed to get away from the other workers.

Trent, however, didn't share his concern. "You didn't tell me you were bringing in other guys."

"I tell you what you need to know," Hunter replied, confirming that they were now far enough away to talk privately. Any further and he'd be outside the security booth, and that wasn't exactly the kind of place for this type of discussion.

"Look, we need to get this together," Trent said. "I didn't sign up for this, you know."

"I really don't care what you *signed up* for," Hunter said. "You're in this now. You've got to see it through."

"That's what I'm saying. I don't think I can do this."

"I don't think you have a choice," Hunter said.

"It's too late to go back now. Do that, and you'll be sharing a cell with Fischer. No. Better yet, I'll make sure it's Ray. He seems like the type that will hold a grudge. And a shiv."

Trent was actually taken aback. Physically. He took two steps back, he was so in shock over the direct threat. Hunter knew he was playing it too rough with the guy. Trent wasn't the type that handled this kind of pressure well. That was evidently clear. But Hunter didn't have time for handholding. He needed to get moving. There was no way to let Chavo and Batista know that he was being delayed.

Hunter left Trent behind and headed for the security booth in the front corner of the warehouse. The room stood out from the rest of the offices due to a glass wall that ran from the floor to the ceiling. The huge expanse of dark-tinted glass sent the message that even though the workers couldn't see into the room, Ray had no problem keeping an eye on them. Hunter had to give the guy props for his ideas. Ray was like the Cerebral Security, the way he planned everything out so well.

The booth was also the only office in the place that had had its door closed from the moment Hunter first entered the joint. This helped keep the workers aware of its presence, but backed off enough to let Ray do his job without interruption. Hunter had noticed that

Ray and one other guard were always on duty at the warehouse, and the booth was manned at all times. He wasn't going to be able to just pull Ray out for another tour. He was busy coming up with a plan in his mind as he knocked on the door.

A guard that Hunter had not been introduced to yet opened the door to him.

"Mind if I come in?" Hunter asked.

"Sorry, sir," the guard replied. "Security only."

He looked over the guard's shoulder and saw Ray sitting at a computer. "Yo, Ray, tell this guy I'm cool. I need to talk to you."

Ray looked up from the screen. Hunter could almost see the guy doing calculations in his head. When this whole operation started up, Ray would probably have never let the new guy into the security booth once, much less twice in as many days. But the Ray that Hunter had met this morning was over Fischer's whole deal. Hunter hoped that this would work to his advantage.

"Let him in," Ray said with a shrug.

"Thanks, man," Hunter said as he stepped inside. The security booth was over twice the size of his office, but with half the space. A bank of video screens covered the wall that ran perpendicular to the tinted glass. Cameras monitored activity everywhere, both in and out of the warehouse. Even the bathrooms were monitored, though the stalls, thankfully, were free from spying eyes. He couldn't help but notice that the desk had been positioned in such a way that Ray could keep one eye on the tinted window and the other on the monitors at all times.

To call it a "desk," though, was an understatement. Ray was sitting behind a huge security console with two computer workstations for him and whatever guard was on duty. The rest of the console had controls for what Hunter assumed were the cameras and alarm system. The whole thing was about the size of the light and soundboard for a small arena.

"What's up?" Ray asked as he turned to Hunter.

Hunter was distracted for a moment. He thought he heard a radio playing, but quickly realized it was a police scanner monitoring all activity in the Brooklyn area. Ray clearly knew what he was doing. As Hunter took stock of the room, he could see Chavo and Batista on a screen on the top row.

"Impressive set up," Hunter said, bringing his attention back to Ray. "Meant to say that yesterday."

"Thanks."

Hunter then looked at the other guard. He had returned to his position and wasn't bothering to hide the fact that he was looking directly at the screen with Chavo and Batista on it.

"You got a minute to talk?" Hunter asked Ray.

"Sure," Ray said, getting up. "You wanna go outside so we don't bother Jimmy?"

Hunter looked at the guard, then at the glass window. *No. I don't want that at all.* "Well, it's kind of private," Hunter said, making up his plan as he went along. "Something I'd rather not talk about out in the open."

Ray looked at Hunter and then at the guard, Jimmy. Once again he just shrugged his shoulders and motioned for Jimmy to give them a minute. The guard got up and left the room without a word.

"First of all," Hunter said. "I'm sorry about earlier. I didn't know bringing in new guys was gonna cause trouble."

"Not your fault," Ray said. "Fischer likes things to run smoothly more than he worries about security. Until things don't run so smoothly, that is. Then there's hell to pay for any breakdown in security."

"Sounds like you're ready to move on," Hunter said, looking at the monitor. On the screen he saw Chavo checking his watch. They were going to move soon.

"Ready to retire's more like it," Ray said.

"Amen to that," Hunter said.

"Look, don't worry about it," Ray said dismissively.

"There's something else," Hunter said, but then stopped like he was reluctant to talk about it.

"Go on," Ray prodded.

Hunter took a step over to the tinted glass window. "Come here for a second." Ray got up and joined him at the window. From where he stood, Hunter could see right into Trent's office. The guy was working at his computer, but kept looking up like he knew he was being watched. "What do you think of Trent?" Hunter asked.

"He's an okay guy," Ray said. "Pretty much keeps to himself. Never got much of a read off him. Why?"

"He makes me nervous," Hunter said, throwing a glance back to the monitor. Chavo and Batista were gone from the break room. He could see them in the monitor that was tied to the storage room with the back door. They were moving too slow for Hunter. He knew they had to be careful not to trip the alarm, but he wouldn't be able to keep Ray's attention forever.

"I thought Trent was a friend of yours. He did bring you into the fold."

"I don't put blind trust in my friends," Hunter said. "I've been burned too many times." That part was true. He couldn't even count the number of times one of his allies had turned against him in the ring. But he had to hold back a smile when he remembered all the times he had surprised a *supposed* friend himself.

"What's he done?"

Hunter acted like he was thinking about the question. He didn't want to call too much attention to Trent. The guy might go over the edge if Ray ever questioned him directly. Still, it would be useful to distract Ray with the suspicion. Since Trent's job for the NSA had effectively ended when he got Hunter into the building, it wasn't like Ray could catch him doing anything.

"It's nothing specific," Hunter said. "He just seems . . . excessively nervous."

Ray took in what "Mike" was saying and nodded in agreement. "Yeah, I noticed that too. Trent used to be cool as a cucumber . . . but lately, I don't know."

Hunter checked the monitor. Batista was pulling the equipment bag up from the tunnel. *Just another minute.*

"I don't want to cause trouble," Hunter said. "I just noticed a change in him from the last time we worked together." Now that he had put suspicion on Trent, he knew he had to dial it back. Hunter had hoped that Trent was a nervous character by nature. It made sense that he'd be more anxious since going to the NSA, but nothing about the guy suggested that he had ever been "cool as a cucumber," or any other produce for that matter.

"I noticed it too," Ray said.

"Look, there's so much going on with the move

tomorrow," Hunter said, backing down. "It could be that. I don't want to look like some snitch or anything. But I'm gonna keep an eye on him for you."

"Thanks, man," Ray said as they moved back to his desk.

Hunter checked the monitor. Chavo and Batista were back in the break room, and their equipment bag was nowhere to be seen. They had managed to slip in the necessary materials to bug the phone, tap into the security monitors to make duplicate recordings, and hack into the computer. Now it was just a matter of doing all that while Ray and his guard kept a close eye on the monitors. The job was far from done.

chapter
twelve

Torrie watched as Masterson speared the strawberry
with his long silver fork. He lifted it up to the steaming pot of dark and white chocolate. She could feel
the heat from the melted chocolate. The mixture
smelled divine. Masterson carefully dipped the lus-
cious strawberry into the decadent chocolate, making
sure to get an equal coating of dark and white. Then
he raised the dipped strawberry toward Torrie's
mouth, but stopped inches from her face. Taking the
invitation, Torrie leaned forward, opening her red-
painted lips and taking the strawberry into her mouth.
Slowly, she bit down on the chocolate-covered straw-

berry. The warm chocolate mixed with cool straw-berry was a burst of flavor in her mouth. Finally, she raised her eyes to meet Masterson's and knew she had him right where she wanted him. "Delicious," she said, looking directly at him.

"Yes, you are, Larkin," Masterson said as he took the fork away from her.

When Torrie had accepted his invitation out for dessert at one of his latest acquisitions, she hadn't ex-pected a fondue restaurant. The place was a little pre-tentious for her tastes. On the other hand, she was happy that her work allowed her to go off her diet. Though with each bite of chocolate decadence she promised herself an extra set in the weight room.

"I'm having a wonderful time," Torrie said as she returned the favor and prepared a strawberry for Masterson's enjoyment. "This place is such a kitschy throwback."

"I know," Masterson said as he took a small bite from the chocolate-dipped strawberry. "These restau-rants that specialize in one thing or another are all the rage lately. Good money makers."

"I'll say." Torrie looked at the small fondue restau-rant. The place was as busy as Magma had been the night before. The New York elite were quick to fol-low any trend. And they were just as quick to move on to the next. "Moneymakers" like this place and

Magma had short shelf lives, as far as Torrie could tell. Of course, investing in them worked perfectly for Masterson. The police would become interested in Masterson's less reputable business dealings just at the point the trendsters moved onto the new hip and happening place. He'd close down the restaurant and shift his money laundering to the next hot spot, forcing any investigation to start again from scratch. She didn't doubt the guy knew how to play the system.

Nor did she doubt that she knew how to play him.

"I'm getting kind of full," Torrie said. They had already dined on apples in a rich cheese sauce and toasted marshmallows over the open flame. Though Torrie still had plenty of room for actual food, she also wanted to get things moving along. A fondue restaurant was a cute novelty, but it didn't exactly encourage a quick meal. "What do you say we send the rest of the strawberries to your friends over there and get out of here."

Masterson covered the surprise on his face. "I didn't realize you noticed my . . . *friends*. Part of their job is to be unobtrusive on demand."

"What can I say? I'm observant," Torrie said. Even if she hadn't seen the two guys on Hunter's recording from his trip to the warehouse yesterday, they still would have caught Torrie's attention. Aside from their large size, the tattoo on the one guy's face and the impressive amount of silver worn by the other certainly made them noticeable.

"You don't mind, do you?" Masterson asked. "It's just in my line of work, it helps to travel with protection."

"Always a good idea," Torrie said. "But I hope they don't follow you everywhere."

"Not at all," Masterson said as he got up from his chair and held a hand out to her. "You wanted to go home?"

"Go?" Torrie said. "Yes. But I never said anything about *home.*"

Masterson's smile told her that she was in. "Well, then, I have quite a selection of wines at my home."

"That sounds lovely," Torrie said as they walked out of the restaurant. Torrie saw Masterson wave off the bodyguards. She had assumed they would follow and wait around outside, which would make the evening considerably more difficult for her. But Masterson probably realized that it would make things more difficult for him as well. She was glad to have earned his trust so quickly.

Masterson helped Torrie into his town car. She made sure to flash him enough of her thigh as she sat back into the car to give him a hope for how the evening would progress. Having already agreed to go back to his place, she figured his imagination was already going the direction she had intended.

As Masterson moved around to the other side of the car to get in, Torrie settled into the plush leather seating. She said hi to the driver, but he only nodded without even bothering to look back at her. Suddenly, Torrie didn't feel so proud of herself for getting Masterson to give his bodyguards the night off. Considering the size of the guy in the front seat, it looked like Masterson was under protection everywhere he went. Hopefully the driver would stay in the car when they got back to Masterson's place. She didn't need an audience for what she had to do later.

"Home," Masterson said as he settled in beside her. The driver nodded and pulled the car out into the street. Torrie suspected that any number of things could happen to her in the back of this limo, and the driver would keep looking ahead. Considering the hulking mass of a man in front of her, she doubted the opposite was true. If she tried to pull anything on Masterson while his driver was near, she suspected the driver's attention would quickly turn in her direction.

"That was an amazing restaurant," Torrie enthused. "I can't wait . . ."

The ring from Masterson's cell phone cut her off. This was the fifth time it had happened over the course of the evening. As he had with the other calls, Masterson held up an apologetic hand and answered. The conversation was in short clips, with very little information Torrie could make out, again, like all the others.

"Sorry about that," Masterson said as he ended the call and slipped it back into his jacket.

Torrie slid across the leather toward Masterson. "I'm beginning to think you're more interested in your little toy than me."

"Never," Masterson said, warming to the attention.

"Really?" Torrie asked as her hand slid across his chest. "I don't think I believe you. I think you can't go a full minute without your phone."

"I most certainly can," Masterson said. "When given the proper motivation."

"Such as?"

"I think you know."

Torrie leaned in closer, pressing her body against his. She slid her right hand under his jacket while her left hand was busy elsewhere. Reaching deep, she felt the warm metal of his phone and pulled it out of his pocket. "Let's see," she said playfully as she pulled away from him and slid back across the seat. "Shall I time you?"

"Very funny, Larkin," he said. "Now give back the phone."

"Just a second," Torrie said, waving him off. "This is one seriously tricked-out phone. Where did you get it?"

"It was a gift," Masterson said. "Now please give it back."

"Does it have a camera?" Torrie asked suggestively as she pressed some buttons, bringing up the menu. She scrolled down the long list of features, looking for the call history.

"Larkin," Masterson said stiffly as he reached across the seat. Torrie considered playing with him some more, but there was something in his tone that told her this game was not going to get what she wanted.

"Okay," she said as she handed back the phone. "If I knew you were going to be this much fun, I wouldn't have left my boyfriend."

"I'm sorry," Masterson said. "The phone can be . . . temperamental."

Not just the phone, Torrie thought.

As if it knew it needed to break the tension, the damn phone rang yet again. Torrie let out a petulant huff as Masterson answered it.

Masterson was still on the phone when they reached their destination. His "home" in the Upper East Side was an apartment in one of the newest-looking buildings in the area. Torrie had already known all about his penthouse apartment from her mission brief, but she still acted surprised and impressed by the luxurious look of the building as they pulled up. The act was totally wasted on Masterson, though; he was still deep in his phone conversation.

"No, I don't intend to be there," Masterson said. "I'll be at Champagne tomorrow night." Torrie's ears perked up at the mention of tomorrow night. That was when the meth shipment was coming in. It wasn't a surprise that Masterson didn't plan on being there, but it did make the call much more interesting to her. At first she thought it was odd to say that he'd be "at champagne," until she realized Champagne was the name of another one of his recent trendy acquisitions.

Torrie continued listening as she stepped out of the car first. She waited as Masterson slid across the street with the phone still attached to his ear. Again, the chauffer remained at his post, though even from behind Torrie could see he was keeping a vigilant eye on the street. She left the limo behind as they headed for the entrance.

"Hold on," Masterson said into the phone. "Larkin, do you mind if we stay out here for a minute? I always lose calls when I go into the lobby."

"Sure," Torrie said, allowing herself to sound disappointed to be kept waiting. Luckily for Masterson this wasn't a real date, or she would have dumped his ass long ago. Instead, Torrie occupied herself by studying the other buildings on the street. Compared to the place Masterson lived, they weren't very interesting, but it was a good way to cover the fact that she was still listening intently to Masterson's conversation in the hope of gaining some tidbit of information.

The conversation stretched on for a couple minutes. It was by far the longest he had been on the phone all night. His end of the talk was little more than "Yes," "No," and "I'm open to the possibility." Other than the mention of Champagne, the one interesting phrase she heard was, "The timing has to be perfect," but that didn't really tell her much of anything.

She was turning her attention to look into the lobby of Masterson's building when she noticed a group of teen boys walking in their direction. They looked somewhat out of place for the upscale neighborhood in their dark T-shirts and shredded jeans. But as they got closer, Torrie noticed it was all a front—an extravagantly expensive attempt to look more street than they actually were. She relaxed as they passed. The stares they shot her way were typical of the teenage male when seeing a woman who looked like Torrie. It was doubtful they were part of her fan base.

That is, until she saw what seemed to be a look of recognition on one of the boys' faces. Even with her darker hair, she knew she still couldn't hide certain familiar attributes. Torrie turned back toward the building, allowing her brown wig to conceal her face and hoping to distract the boy with the tightness of her dress. At first she thought the move had worked as the teens continued past. She could feel their stares on her, but she was used to that. It was nothing compared to the looks she got while waiting backstage before she went out for a Bra and Panties match.

It wasn't until she heard the boy loudly say, "I'm telling you, it's her," that she started to grow concerned.

chapter
thirteen

Torrie quickly took stock of the situation.

Masterson was still distracted by his call and showing no sign he was wrapping it up anytime soon. Luckily, he didn't seem to notice the teens at all.

"Dude, you're out of your mind," one of the kids said. They were still walking away, but their pace had slowed noticeably.

Torrie considered her options. She could tell Masterson that she was cold and would wait for him inside, if it weren't for the fact that it was a perfect seasonably warm night. She could go with the old bathroom excuse, if only she hadn't used it toward the middle of the meal to report in to Thompson and confirm she was probably going back to Masterson's place. Of course she could always just grow bored and walk inside, but she didn't want to risk annoying him any more than she already had with her little phone game.

"Here," the surprisingly observant rich kid said. "I'll show you."

Out of the corner of her eye, Torrie saw the group turn and head back in her direction. The annoying observant kid was leading the pack. She was sure she could talk her way out of the situation, considering that the idea of a WWE Superstar using a false name to ensnare an international crime lord seemed ridiculous at best. But Torrie didn't want to risk any kind of suspicion from Masterson. Just the question that her name might not be Larkin was enough to set a guy like him off.

"It's best we don't be seen together until then," Masterson said. It finally sounded like he was about to end the call, but it was too late. The boys were almost on them. Torrie started moving for the door to the building.

"Hey," one of the kids said.

Suddenly, the chauffeur's arm shot out across the pavement in front of the boys, stopping them from getting any closer to their boss. Torrie hadn't even heard the driver get out of the limo. It didn't matter. She chalked it up to good fortune, grabbed Masterson's arm as he ended his call, and let him pull her into the building. She didn't hear the exchange between the chauffeur and kids, but it didn't matter. She was just lucky the driver was also a good bodyguard.

Masterson nodded to the doorman who was supposed to be watching the lobby and keeping out the riffraff. The guy didn't even look up from his magazine. It looked a bit to Torrie like he was asleep, in fact. A guy with that kind of a work ethic in a building like this probably wasn't long for his job. In the meantime, having unobservant security in the building could work to Torrie's advantage.

Masterson used his key to call the elevator. That wasn't a surprise. Torrie knew that high-rise buildings like this one didn't just open their elevator doors to anyone. She suspected that every entrance, stairwell, hall, and elevator had a security camera trained on it. But if the screens were supposed to be watched by the unobservant guy at the door, she certainly wasn't about to bring it up.

"The penthouse?" Torrie asked, trying to sound impressed even though she had known where they were going all along.

It was clear that her tone had done its job on

Masterson. "I hope you don't think it's too showy. I couldn't turn the place down once I saw the view."

"I totally understand," Torrie said as if she totally did.

"Top floor," Masterson said as the elevator opened. They stepped out into the short hall, and Masterson opened his door, ushering Torrie inside.

The penthouse was just how Torrie imagined it would be; all sleek lines and modern furniture in stainless steel and black. What the place lacked in warmth it made up for in testosterone, but not the type that Torrie was used to. This was a kind of retro metrosexual, a throwback to the sixties with a twenty-first-century flair. It looked about as comfortable as a morgue.

But the view was another matter entirely. Floor-to-ceiling windows opened out the living room to Manhattan at night. Torrie was caught off guard by the beauty of the city at night with its tall towers lighting up the sky. She could understand why anyone would spend what he did for the place. She had certainly never seen anything like this growing up in Boise.

"Nice place," Torrie said breathlessly as she slipped off her heels and made herself comfortable on the black leather couch.

"It serves its purpose," Masterson said as he opened up the bar.

"And what purpose is that?"

"You'll have to wait and see."

It was all Torrie could do not to gag at his oh-so-smooth lines.

Torrie watched intently as Masterson mixed a pair of martinis for them and brought the drinks to the couch. On any other date she would have been offended that he didn't even bother to ask her what she wanted. From where she sat, she could tell the bar was well stocked enough to handle almost any request. But Torrie ignored the lack of manners as they raised their glasses in a silent toast. Torrie brought the drink to her lips, pausing to confirm that Masterson was indeed going to drink his and then taking a demure little sip of her own.

As the cool martini slid down her throat, she kept her eyes locked on Masterson. She put down her glass and used her now-free hand to trace a finger along his jawline. Continuing down to his shoulder and his arm, she took his glass out of his hand and put it down on the coffee table. Still looking directly into his eyes, she pushed the tiny button on her ring that sent a stream of clear liquid into his glass. At the same time, she distracted him with a kiss.

Masterson kissed back hungrily. His hands started exploring her body, quickly going places where they weren't exactly welcome. Torrie was silently thankful for his desperate aggression. It made it easier to push him away. With a smile, she took her glass and lifted it to her lips as if she was only delaying the inevitable. Masterson mirrored her move by taking his own glass. This time, Torrie took a much longer sip and was rewarded when Masterson nearly finished his drink.

After they both put their glasses back down, Torrie responded to his earlier moves, giving him a look that said, "You may proceed." And he did just that. He proceeded to pass out on the couch, thanks to the sedative in his drink.

"Thompson said that stuff was fast," she mumbled to herself. "He wasn't kidding."

Torrie left him drowsing on the couch and went in search of his computer. It only took opening a couple doors to get to the office. As far as she knew, this was the furthest any government agent had gotten into Masterson's place before. Her nervousness was mixed with a little pride. The computer was sitting on the desk in front of her in sleep mode. All it took was for her to wake it with the touch of one key, and the job was halfway done.

Torrie slipped her hand in her purse and pulled out her compact. Far from it being time to reapply, she pressed down on the lid, and two small metal connectors popped out of either end of the case. She didn't need to compare the connector size to see that the one on the right side of the compact would do the trick. Torrie slipped the connector into the computer port and waited. The cute little piece of NSA technology would do the rest for her.

chapter
fourteen

Vince was the first to arrive at the temporary headquarters in the hotel gym on Friday morning. He
had even beaten the pissant receptionist flunky that
usually stood guard. Vince had a full schedule of
meetings that day, but that wasn't the reason for his
early arrival. Thompson had made the calls for this
meeting long after midnight last night. The tone in
his voice had set Vince's suspicions on edge, but
Thompson refused to discuss anything over the
phone. Considering that Vince knew they were both
on cell phones with the latest in anti-eavesdropping
technology, it was clear that Thompson didn't have

security concerns. He was just blowing Vince off.

Vince planned to have a word with the man before the Superstars showed for the meeting. He'd had enough of Thompson's games. *Nobody* kept Vincent Kennedy McMahon out of the loop. Especially when it came to his wrestlers. It was time for them to have the talk that they both had been putting off for years. It didn't take him long to realize that Thompson was thinking the same thing, but coming at it from a different angle, because the normally punctual NSA director was curiously late for the meeting.

As the clock ticked past the hour, Vince welcomed his team as they came in one by one. They had been instructed to vary their times of arrival so all five of them weren't getting on and off the elevator at the same time to head to a place that was supposed to be closed for renovations. Vince remained in the lobby, hoping to get a word with Thompson beforehand, but doubting it was going to happen more with every passing minute.

"Hey, Vince," John Cena said as he entered. He was the last of the Superstars to arrive. His workload had been intentionally light for this mission, as he had some promotional appearances to make around the city related to his movie work. Vince never worried that John was stretching himself too thin. Working for the WWE was several full-time jobs, and he expected nothing less than one hundred percent from all his Superstars.

"Got a second?" the wrestler/rapper/actor asked.

Vince looked out to the hallway. It was still empty. "Looks like I do," he said.

"About Monday night's *Raw*," Cena said. "I was looking over the schedule and wondering?"

"Yeah," Vince said, already knowing where the question was going.

"What is it?"

"What's what?"

"Come on, Vince," Cena said.

"Well, now," Vince said. "Why should I spoil the surprise? You'll know in plenty of time to get ready."

"So I'm in the final match?"

"Possibly," Vince said with a sly smile. The reason for that smile was he had also just seen Thompson coming down the hall. "Now go in back with the others. We've got other work to take care of at the moment."

Cena shook his head in resignation, but did as he was told. That was another good thing about the kid; he took direction well.

Most of the time.

"Mornin', Vince," Thompson said as he came into the lobby. His little lackey followed him and took the usual position behind the reception desk. Not for the first time, Vince was reminded of the Briscos. He put the association out of his mind as Thompson tried to brush past him. Vince had had tougher opponents try that move before, and he quickly countered it as if he had anticipated it all along. His hand shot out and grabbed Thompson by the shoulder gently but firmly. "I was hoping we could have a word," Vince said.

"Love to, but the team's waiting," Thompson replied lightly. "I would have been here sooner, but I was on a call with Washington."

"Care to tell me what the call was about?" Vince asked.

"Not particularly."

Vince didn't like that answer. "Why do I think you're keeping something from me?"

"Vince, old buddy," Thompson said with a forced laugh, "I'm keeping many things from you. You know your clearance only goes so far."

"That's not what I meant," Vince said. "I'm talking about this team. *My* team. I want to know what's going on here."

"Well, let's get the meeting started so you can find out," Thompson said as he pushed his way past.

Vince did not like this at all. Phil Thompson hadn't had Vince's trust when they knew each other over forty years ago. Thompson hadn't had it when they made this little arrangement two years earlier. He hadn't managed to earn in the time since. If anything, he was losing what little faith there had been with this current mission. Vince kept his guard up as he followed Thompson into the back. His Superstars were all seated on the exercise equipment again, in roughly the same positions as yesterday.

Vince had only seen each of them briefly the night before when they reported in. Hunter, Chavo, and Batista reported at midnight just after getting out of the warehouse. They weren't expected back there until that evening for the all-night move. They turned over the information Chavo had hacked from Fischer's computers and then turned in for the evening. Torrie showed up shortly thereafter with her own little hacking device full of Masterson's files. Thompson had been pleased by the success when they parted company. That pleasure had left Thompson's voice when he called Vince at three o'clock, requesting the meeting.

"I'd like to congratulate you all on a job well done," Thompson said as a greeting when he got back to the weight room. Vince stayed in the doorway, surveying the scene. "Our analysts were up all night going through the information you pulled off the computers. We have more than enough evidence to indict Garrett Fischer, intercept his shipment tonight, and take everyone into custody," Thompson continued. "By this time tomorrow his operation will be entirely shut down."

Vince could see his Superstars were rightfully proud of their efforts.

"What about the tapes we pulled from the security cameras and the phone conversations?" Hunter asked.

"Nothing really there," Thompson said. "But it laid some good groundwork. When you go back tonight, I have something else for you to sneak in. It's a transmitter you can link into the surveillance system. That way when we're about to start the raid, we can see exactly what Fischer's camera sees."

"No can do," Batista said. "No transmissions in or out of the building."

"Which is why we'll need you to disable that part of the system before we move in."

"Not asking for much, are you?" Chavo asked.

"Hey, you wanted to play with the big boys," Thompson said. "Now it's time for you to step up."

"Was that a height joke?" Chavo asked, lightly. "Because I think that was a height joke."

But Thompson didn't have time for jokes. "Hunter, you said Fischer needed some more guys for tonight?"

"Yeah," Hunter replied. "Low profile. Just a few to handle loading the trucks at the docks. They won't be going back to the warehouse or dealing with the toxic waste part. Fischer doesn't want anyone to be connected to the shipment out of the port except for the truck drivers, me, and Trent."

"I've got a few roadies we can use," Vince said. A few members of the traveling stage crew had been brought into the fold for just such occasions. They didn't receive the full training that the Superstars did, but it was helpful to have extra hands around when necessary. Considering they'd be done with the load-in at the Garden by early afternoon, he figured he could spare a few from setup for the mission.

"Great," Thompson said. "You guys have done a great job."

Vince didn't like the way Thompson was speaking with such finality. It seemed to Vince that there was a loose end going unmentioned. He wasn't about to weaken his position by being the one to bring it up. He had faith in his Superstars. Without missing a beat, Hunter was the one that finally spoke for the team. "That's great. But what about Masterson?"

"Unfortunately, there was nothing to tie Dietrich Masterson to Garrett Fischer," Thompson said.

"You mean aside from the fact that I saw the two of them together the other day," Hunter said. "And the video you have to prove that."

"Unfortunately, that's not substantial proof of

anything," Thompson said. "The files you took off Fischer's server were the keys to the kingdom. But only Fischer's kingdom."

"There's *no* mention of Masterson in the files?" Batista asked.

"Exactly," Thompson said. "And without that proof, I don't want to risk losing Fischer on anything else."

"The analysts went through all the stuff from Fischer's server?" Chavo asked. "Looked to me like there were a lot of files."

"Everything," Thompson said. "There was a document titled 'Lockbox,' but it was empty."

"So maybe that file was too secure for your little hacking device to get into," Hunter said. "Maybe that's the smoking gun. Chavo can go back in tonight while he's waiting for the shipment to arrive."

"Be careful," Thompson said. "I don't want to risk losing Fischer."

"Excuse me," Torrie chimed in. "But what about the files I took off Masterson's computer? Wasn't there anything useful?"

"The menus for his restaurants," Thompson said dismissively. "And some personal correspondence to his mother. You must have fallen for a dummy computer."

"That was the only computer in the place," Torrie

said defensively. "While everything downloaded into that little device you gave me, I did a thorough sweep. Used everything I learned from my training to trace out from the power sources. Aside from a ridiculously expensive entertainment system, there wasn't any other noticeable technology in the place. Maybe he's got a secret office in the building? Close, but not too close."

"Either way, it's too dangerous for you to go back," Thompson said. "Masterson has to have been suspicious when he woke up and found you were gone."

"I can cover," Torrie said with no question in her voice.

"Too risky," Thompson said.

"Doesn't sound like you got much faith in us," Batista said, putting a voice to Vince's main concern.

"I said you all did a good job, and I meant it," Thompson said. "Sometimes we have to let the bad guy get away. It doesn't mean we're not keeping track of him. It's just that none of you will be involved. This is the nature of our agreement. You guys are my hit-and-run team. Get in. Get out. Get it done. If you can't get it done, we move on. I believe you have a long trip down to Houston next week?"

"That's next week," Hunter said. "We've still got time to 'get it done' here."

"And we've got someone on the inside," Chavo said as he laid a hand on Torrie's shoulder. "We can use that."

"The decision has been made," Thompson said with a note of finality and condescension. "You're agents of the NSA now. Take your orders and do as you are told."

It was clear that all five members of the team did not like that. Hunter was about to speak when Vince raised a hand. "Enough," he said.

"But Vince—" Cena chimed in. So far he had the least invested in this mission, and even he looked pissed that they were being dismissed so easily.

Vince shot them all down with his signature glare. "I said enough. Hunter, Chavo, and Batista need to focus on their responsibilities at the warehouse, or we may risk alerting Fischer."

"Thank you for seeing it my way," Thompson said.

"I'm sorry," Vince said with no apology in his voice. "Did I say *anything* that indicated I agree with you? I'm doing my job. Now, if you don't mind, I've got some company business to go over with my Superstars." Vince stepped out of the doorway, letting Thompson know that *he* was now dismissed.

Phil Thompson was not a stupid man. He left without another word.

"Vince, I can't believe you let that guy walk all over us," Hunter said once Thompson was gone.

"Who said I did anything of the kind?" Vince said. "What I did was get him the hell out of our hair. You guys get some rest, then go back to the warehouse and do what you can to find out about Masterson. Get into that lockbox file and see what's there. Talk to whoever you can about Masterson. If Trent doesn't know who he is, *someone* there should at least know something. As far as I'm concerned, this mission hasn't changed in the least."

Vince was rewarded with smiles from the team. "And keep Cena in the loop," Vince added. "He's the only backup you guys have got."

All four men nodded.

"Torrie, are you free tonight?" Vince asked.

"Gee, I don't think so, Mister McMahon," she said. "I believe I have a date."

"Glad to hear it," Vince said. "You've got the most important task here. Even if we tie Masterson to the meth lab, I have a feeling that we have a chance to get him for a hell of a lot more. You need to find where Masterson keeps his real files."

"Oh, I think I've got a good idea," she said with a nod and a smile.

Vince looked out at his team. They were all pumped and ready to go. "Well," he said. "Get out of here."

The Superstars sprang out of their seats like they were about to hit the ring. Vince watched with pride as they left headquarters. Vince was damned if the NSA was going to use his Superstars as errand boys. He had signed them up for the big game, and they were going to play their parts.

But Thompson was another matter entirely. Vince had been reluctant to sign up for this job two years ago, but he knew he couldn't let his country down. Vince was a patriot long before it became the vogue. And he was going to do that job, whether or not Thompson had anything to say about it. He still couldn't get over the fact that someone had thought putting Phil Thompson over him was the way to go. Even a total stranger would have had a better chance of convincing him. But, no, the NSA director had to be the one man in Vince's life who ever got the best of him without feeling at least some of Vince's brand of retribution.

chapter
fifteen

Cadet Philip J. Thompson didn't like being in the headmaster's office. Not that he was in trouble. Cadet Thompson never did anything that would even remotely get him in trouble. The honor student was first in his class and a shining example of military elite . . . at least as far as he was concerned. West Point was in his future, and from there he could only imagine the possibilities. Disciplinary problems were not among his chief concerns, and yet he was called in for a disciplinary reason.

Cadet Thompson followed every single rule the school had laid out, even the ones that weren't formally inscribed but rather *implied*. He did so without question day in and day out. But today he did wonder about the logic behind the one that said that students accused of wrongdoing had the right to face their accusers.

"Cadet McMahon," Headmaster Chadsworth Smith III addressed the only other person in the room. "I take it from your silence that you do not grasp the gravity of the situation."

Philip was beside himself with glee. It looked like he was finally going to win. Countless months of torment under Cadet Vincent Kennedy McMahon were about to come to an end. It was pure luck that had put Philip in the right place at the right time. And it was his own adherence to the rules that brought about this situation. The only thing from stopping him from truly enjoying the experience was Cadet McMahon's damned unwillingness to show fear.

The headmaster let out a small sigh and walked around his desk, leaving the room in the first silence since they had entered a half hour earlier. He reached up to the wall and lifted his U.S. Model 1833 dragoon sword down off the silver hooks, holding it on display. The blade was polished so brightly that the overhead light reflected off it and bounced around the room as the weapon came down. Philip had seen the sword many times before, but this was the first time he was about to witness it in action.

Philip had heard about this maneuver before. Rumors of the headmaster's swordplay spread quickly in whispers and snickering among the less reputable students. Even though the sword had become a joke throughout most of the campus, cadets still spoke of its effect. Once the headmaster had the sword in hand, it was usually mere moments before he obtained a confession. Not that the headmaster ever used it on a student. That would certainly bring unwanted attention onto the school. But still, students cowered under the awesome power of the sword. It sent a chill of anticipation through Philip, in spite of the fact that the maneuver seemed a little early in this particular interrogation.

The sword made a whistling sound as it cut through the air. The blade was nowhere near Philip, but he still jumped at the quick movement as the headmaster bandied it about with a mere flick of the wrist.

"I know you couldn't have done this alone," the headmaster said to Cadet McMahon between swings of the sword. Philip hadn't seen any accomplices, but he really didn't care. It was McMahon who had been the thorn in his side.

"No, that's not true," the headmaster corrected himself. "You could have easily pulled it off, Cadet McMahon. This little stunt is beneath you, in fact. So far beneath you that it is clear to me that one of your cohorts was the mastermind behind it. You were just along for the ride."

Philip couldn't believe that it sounded like the headmaster was about to let McMahon off. "Sir," he interrupted. "I saw—"

"Did I give you permission to speak, cadet?" The headmaster cut the sword in Philip's direction, sending him back into his chair even though he was still feet from the blade.

"Sorry, sir," Philip said, looking down at his neatly pressed pants. He wasn't used to being addressed in that manner. Certainly not from the headmaster, at least. The more senior cadets often liked to pull rank on him, but never anyone in real power.

It was then that Cadet McMahon chose to speak. "You can put that toy away."

Philip nearly choked in his shock at what McMahon had dared to say. Even the headmaster seemed startled by the audacity of the young cadet.

"Everyone knows that little trick of yours, and it's not going to work on me," Cadet McMahon continued. "I have nothing to confess, so you're not making me nervous by twirling that thing around. You might as well put it away."

The sword stopped, but remained aimed threateningly at Cadet McMahon. For a brief moment, Philip thought the headmaster was actually going to go through with it and use it on the cadet.

"Cadet McMahon, I assure you this is no joking manner," Headmaster Smith barked at him. "Unless you tell me right now who helped you rig the student elections, you will be expelled immediately!"

Philip did his best to keep the look of glee off his face. When he had turned McMahon in, he had never imagined the cadet would be expelled. The best Philip had hoped for would be a week of bathroom duty. That would have more than made up for McMahon's little prank last week of locking Philip out of the dorms in the freezing rain in the middle of the night . . . in his underwear. But to be expelled meant a formal court-martial, a reading of all of McMahon's transgressions, and then his final departure from the school.

At first Philip worried that the punishment did not fit the crime. Sure he wanted McMahon gone, but not at the expense of the headmaster abusing school policy. That wouldn't be right. But then Philip realized where the headmaster was heading. Cadet McMahon would surely be punished for his actions in rigging the election, but the real trouble came from not giving up his partners. To ignore a direct question from any teacher, much less the headmaster, was going against one of the core tenets of the Fishburne Academy Code of Honor. Failure to respond was simply not an option. Any infraction against the Code of Honor led to immediate dismissal.

Headmaster Chadsworth Smith III slammed the sword down on his desk. "Cadet McMahon, I am asking you a *direct* question. And I am ordering you to answer me. Name the person or persons who helps you disrupt the school election."

"Has anyone told Chadsworth Sucks the Third that he won yet?" Cadet McMahon asked, appearing unmoved by the headmaster's threatening tone in the slightest. "I don't even know the guy, but I'd like to congratulate him."

"Cadet McMahon! Your accomplices! Now!"

Philip could see that the prank, combined with McMahon's attitude, had angered Headmaster Smith like nothing before. The headmaster was a disciplinarian, but he never raised his voice and certainly never lost his composure. He was doing both right now. Philip wondered what it was about Cadet McMahon that could get such a rise out of the headmaster. Surely he had met arrogant students before.

Philip encountered nothing *but* arrogance from his peers on a daily basis.

He hadn't been able to believe his luck when he saw Cadet McMahon stuffing one of the three ballot boxes stationed around campus. Philip had quickly run to the headmaster to report what he had seen. Then it was like Christmas and his birthday all rolled into one when it turned out that an overwhelming number of votes from all three boxes had been found to be for Chadsworth Sucks III.

"Cadet McMahon, I do not think you are taking this seriously," the headmaster said.

"I assure you, sir, that is not the case," Cadet McMahon said. "I am very serious about not giving up my friends."

"You realize that you are leaving me no choice," the headmaster said. "Do you not wish to say anything in your defense?"

"Well, I was wondering," McMahon said. "Can I use your phone?"

Philip couldn't have heard him right. That was all he could say at a time like this? Apparently Philip wasn't the only one confused, because the headmaster also asked for a clarification. "Did you just ask me for a phone?"

"Yes, sir," McMahon said. "I need to call my parents to let them know I need a ride home."

Philip was so taken aback by McMahon's arrogance that he barely realized that he had won. McMahon was out. Expelled. Gone. Philip was so beside himself with joy that the next few minutes were a blur. But it wasn't long before McMahon was dismissed to pack his bags.

"Cadet Thompson," the headmaster said once McMahon had left the room. "You look very pleased with yourself."

"No, sir," Philip replied quickly by rote.

"You're not glad to see Cadet McMahon gone?"

Philip wasn't sure how to answer that one. The obvious answer was yes, he was quite pleased. But more of an explanation was required.

"Permission to speak freely, sir?"

"Granted."

"I am happy to see any cadet leave who cannot adhere to our Code of Honor."

"So you think it would be honorable to squeal on his friends?" the headmaster asked. "Over nothing more than a simple prank?"

"The code is clear, sir," Philip said, slightly confused. "He was dishonoring you by ignoring your questions. Your orders."

"True," the headmaster said. "But you should consider that honor is not always something that can adhere to a simple code."

•   •   •

Forty-four years later, the headmaster's words still echoed in Phil Thompson's mind as he headed back to the NSA's New York office. Once again he knew that he was betraying Vince McMahon by not telling him the full story. But he just couldn't risk it. Some truths were more important than honor, and the more people who knew this "truth," the more dangerous things were for everyone involved. Sometimes honor needed to be overlooked in the name of the greater good. Thompson had learned a lot about honor since graduating from Fishburne. Unfortunately, none of those lessons eased his guilt now.

chapter
sixteen

The warehouse was buzzing with activity as Hunter took one last sweep of the place. He knew that all the activity would be a useful distraction. Batista still needed to hook the transmitter up to the security cameras, and Chavo hadn't had a chance to try hacking back into the network yet. Hunter wasn't sure how they were going to disable the scrambler that was blocking transmissions, but that was their problem. Hunter had other things to worry about. He just wanted to take stock one last time before he left to make sure there wouldn't be any surprises for the NSA assault team.

Batista was keeping a watchful eye over the work-men as they carefully moved the waste out to the staging area. The move was happening earlier than Hunter wanted, but Fischer had insisted, and to put it off for no reason would only rouse suspicion. As least he was able to choose an area where everything looked like it was ready to ship out, but was also out of harm's way. The last thing they needed was a stray shot to hit any of the barrels when the NSA raided the warehouse. The area served the added bonus of being next to the security booth. Later Batista could use the cover of the barrels to cut into the security system through the breaker box outside the booth. Not that he was crazy about the idea of using toxic waste as a cover.

Hunter continued his tour by heading back to his office, where Chavo had set up shop earlier. "How's it going?"

"We got good news and bad news," Chavo said. "The good news is, I didn't miss anything on the ini-tial hack yesterday."

"Well, that's not so much *good* news as it's just news, but whatever," Hunter said. "Let me guess the bad. You can't get into this lockbox file."

"Yep," Chavo said. "But at least I was able to find it." Chavo swiveled the laptop around so Hunter could see the screen. There was a square icon with a keyhole in the center and the word LOCKBOX underneath. Hunter rolled his finger along the laptop's track pad and clicked on the icon. Nothing happened.

"The file's password-protected," Chavo explained.

"I thought the whole system was password-protected," Hunter said. "Didn't stop you from getting anything else."

"This is different," Chavo said. "The is unique to Fischer's computer. The code has to be punched in from there."

"That sounds like a level of security beyond what he's set up for," Hunter said. "Seems to me like something Masterson could be behind."

"That's what I was thinking."

"Let me check in with Fischer and see if he's going anywhere tonight," Hunter said. "Even if he isn't, there might be a way to do this. If you can keep Fischer off the computer for a while, you can switch out my laptop for his so that no one notices it's missing."

"And how are we supposed to keep Fischer off the computer?" Chavo asked.

"Hey, that's your deal," Hunter said. "I can't think of *everything.*"

"Thanks a lot," Chavo said with a chuckle.

Hunter left his office and swung by Fischer's. The boss was sitting at his computer, staring intently at the screen. Hunter figured he was probably playing solitaire. "I'm heading out," Hunter said. "You sure you don't want to come out and keep an eye on things at the docks?"

"What do you think I'm paying you for?" Fischer said in what Hunter suspected was supposed to pass as a joking manner. "So I can stay up all night? It's chilly out there on the water. I'll be right here taking a nap in the back, thank you very much."

It was all Hunter could do not to comment on the guy's crappy work ethic. "Where's Trent? We should get going."

"He already went ahead," Fischer said. "Had some last-minute arrangements to tend to. Couldn't do everything in advance of the operation."

"Don't I know it," Hunter said, though he was trying to keep the concern out of his voice. Trent shouldn't have gone ahead without telling him first. They were supposed to go together. Hunter just chalked it up to Trent's nerves and bid Fischer farewell.

"See you in the morning," Fischer said as Hunter left.

There was one last thing Hunter had to do before he could leave the warehouse. He wasn't about to give up on Masterson yet. Somebody there had to know about the guy. He didn't think he could get that information out of Fischer, but there was one other person who might be willing to talk. And it wasn't something he could leave to Chavo and Batista to do in his absence.

"Hey, Ray, mind if I come in?" Hunter asked as he pushed his way into the security booth. Ray was sitting at his computer, alone in the room. "Where's your backup?"

"Got one guy going with the trucks and another waiting at the dump," Ray said. "It's just me all by my lonesome in here tonight."

Hunter couldn't believe his good fortune. Sure, there were about a dozen big burly guys out in the warehouse who Chavo and Batista would need to work around, but none of them were responsible for security. Hunter knew that people usually just paid attention to what they were assigned to do and didn't usually work any harder than that.

"I had a question that I was gonna ask Fischer, but . . . well . . . he's Fischer and all, so—"

"I hear ya," Ray said with a laugh.

"Anyway, that guy that was here the other day," Hunter said. "The one that blew through your security wearing the fancy duds?" Hunter could see Ray's face darken at the mere suggestion of Masterson. "Is he somebody I need to worry about?"

Ray sat in silence for a moment. It was clear that

he was considering his answer. "Look, Mike, I like you."

"Aw, I like you too, Ray," Hunter said. "But not in that way, you know."

"Very funny. Anyway. You don't want to go messing with that dude. He's big-time trouble. Once he started coming around, this went from a pissy little mom-and-pop shop to some full-fledged *operation*. Now, I ain't complaining about the money I'm making, but I also don't like the risk I'm taking. If you know what I mean."

"So he's been around a while?" Hunter asked. Though this was pretty much confirming his suspicions, there was something nagging him at the back of his mind.

"He's what you call the brains of the operation," Ray said. "He's heavily involved. Comes around all the time to meet with the guys and make sure things are going the right way. Name's Dietrich Masterson, and that's all I'm gonna say about that."

"Why do I think you know more about him?"

"Oh, I know a hellova bunch more about him," Ray said. "But that's all I'm gonna *say* about him."

"I catch your meaning," Hunter said. He didn't need to pump Ray for any more information on the subject. He'd leave that to the NSA boys once everyone was taken in. Maybe Ray would be able to use it to strike a deal of some kind. Hunter hoped he wouldn't see too much prison time, considering he wasn't really actively involved in the drug business. Hunter knew he was coming up with justifications, but Ray was a pretty cool guy. At the same time, there was something about what Ray had said that was bugging Hunter. If only he could put a finger on it. "I'm heading out," he said. "Hold down the fort while I'm gone."

"God speed," Ray said.

Hunter gave him a wave and moved off, but stopped himself before he got too far. "Oh, I almost forgot." Hunter came back into the office, leaning on the security console. "I got my guy Chuck doing some computer upgrades on my laptop," he said. "The system here is good, but I got some ideas on how to make it better. So don't worry if you see him hanging out in my office. He ain't goofing off or anything."

"As long as he's not messing with my system, I don't much care about anything else," Ray said.

That didn't sound much like the guy who got all tense when "Mike" brought in his friends. "Finally gave up, huh?" Hunter guessed.

"Only so much I can do," Ray said. "I take my orders from Fischer."

"Whether or not you agree with them," Hunter added.

"Exactly."

Hunter left through the security entrance and took the short walk to his SUV. He pulled out onto the open road and put a few miles between himself and the warehouse before picking up his cell phone and hitting number 1 on the keypad. Phil Thompson picked up without the phone even ringing once.

"Go," he said.

"C and B are back in," Hunter said. "Couldn't get into the lockbox, but they're gonna try another route. And the cameras should be hooked up before midnight."

"Good," Thompson said. "My people will have the remote ready when the trucks arrive."

"You're not going to the warehouse?" Hunter asked.

"No, I'll be at the dock tracking the shipment from there," Thompson said.

"So, I'll be seeing you soon."

"Not if everything goes according to plan," Thompson said. "Communications is going dark from this point forward."

"Hold on," Hunter said. "Is the chairman there?"

There was a pause. "Yeah."

"Put him on for a second."

Another pause.

"What's up?" Vince asked when he got on the line.

"Just wanted to let you know, we got nothing useful on that other issue," Hunter said. That wasn't entirely true: Ray did have information on Masterson, just nothing he could use at the moment. *Or is there?* Hunter thought as his mind finally made the connection. But since he couldn't do anything about it at the moment, he didn't want to say anything over the phone.

"Gotcha," Vince replied. "Talk to you later."

"Later, man," Hunter said as they disconnected and focused on the road in front of him. He finally pinned down what had been bugging him. If Masterson was behind the upgrade of Fischer's operation and stopped by the warehouse all the time, there was something that didn't make any sense to Hunter.

If Masterson comes by all the time to meet with the guys, he thought, *how come Trent didn't know who the guy was when I asked about him the other day?*

chapter
seventeen

The cabdriver dropped Torrie off in front of Champagne, the latest of the trendy New York hot-spots she'd hit this week. Like Masterson's fondue restaurant and Magma, with its spicy fare, this high-priced bar specialized in one thing: champagne. From simple Mimosas to complex champagne creations, the bar was stocked with the best reserves in the city, all of it from the actual Champagne region of France. Not a sparkling wine in the place, according to the Web site, at least.

The place was so trendy, in fact, that the sign above the door had no name on it. It was a simple neon champagne flute with sparkling neon bubbles drifting out of it—quite subtle in its, pretentiousness, as far as Torrie was concerned. This was the third night in a row she was going to be out until all hours. Not her usual training regimen, but sometimes one job got in the way of the other.

Torrie bypassed the line of tourists and poseurs and went straight for the bouncer, a big, burly guy who looked like he could be the next Superstar if Mister McMahon got a hold of him and whipped him into shape. The ill-fitting expensive suit the guy had squeezed into did nothing to hide his muscular bulk. Torrie wasn't sure what kind of trouble a place like Champagne could attract, but with a guy like this at the door, it certainly wasn't getting in. But all that really mattered to her at the moment was whether or not *she* was getting in. She hadn't arranged ahead to be put on the list. She wanted the element of surprise in her favor.

"Hey, there," she said to the bouncer as she stepped up to the front of the line. She ignored the annoyed stares from the trio of overly perfumed, scantily clad Jersey girls waiting to get in.

"Name?" the bouncer asked as he stared down the cleavage of her tight green dress. Normally, any guy that did this to Torrie would receive a knee to the groin for his troubles, but not tonight. Tonight her cleavage served a purpose.

"What's in a name?" Torrie asked. "My name is Larkin, but Mister Masterson isn't exactly expecting me tonight. I was hoping to surprise him. So I'm sure my name isn't on the list."

"I'm sorry, ma'am," the bouncer said. "But Mister Masterson don't like surprises."

She leaned closer to him. "Yes, Dietrich can be a bit tense. But I assure you, this"—she rubbed her hand down his muscular arm—"is a surprise he won't mind."

"I don't know, ma'am," the bouncer said.

"Hey, we were here first," one of the Jersey girls whined nasally.

"And I'm sure you'll be here last too," Torrie said sweetly back.

Torrie had taken a chance, mentioning Masterson by name. She probably would have gotten in using her most prominent assets alone. But now that she had mentioned Dietrich by name, she put the bouncer on alert. That meant losing the element of surprise, but she was damned if she wasn't going to get in. Time for a new direction.

"Tell you what," she said as she slid her hand over the bouncer's jacket, past what felt like a gun, and to the walkie-talkie clipped to his lapel. "I had wanted to surprise Dietrich, but why don't you call in and check? I promise you, he won't be upset."

Torrie worried that she had lost her touch. Instead of going for the radio, the bouncer was looking past her. It was one thing to send her on her way, it was another to ignore her completely. She turned in the direction of his gaze and saw Masterson's town car parked down the block. The chauffeur's window slid open, and a hand came out, effectively giving her the thumbs-up.

Torrie smiled at the bouncer, waved back to the chauffeur, and sauntered into the club, ignoring the foul mouths of the girls in line giving the bouncer an earful. That level of class was exactly the reason they were in line, and she was inside.

The pretentiousness of Champagne didn't stop at the neon sign. The club interior was all silver and sleek. In many ways it evoked the same feel as Masterson's apartment, causing Torrie to wonder if he used the same decorator for each. The other thing she noticed was that the place was far from standing room only. Not that she was complaining. Torrie wasn't a big fan of packed clubs with wall-to-wall sweaty people shouting to be heard over the DJ du jour. Of course the Jersey girls outside would probably flip out if they ever got in and saw there was no real reason for them to be kept waiting in the first place. That thought made Torrie smile.

Torrie bypassed the bar, though she had several

drink offers along the way from slicked-back men in expensive suits acting like they weren't staring as their eyes followed her through the club. The good thing about places like this was that the men were all the same, desperate not to look desperate and with money to burn. But more importantly, they thought they were so above it all in their white-collar jobs that they never would watch television. She wouldn't be recognized. Even though her fans ran the gamut from blue-collar to blue blood, they were all salt-of-the-earth types, no matter what income bracket. None of them would be seen in this orgy of the ostentatious.

Once past the bar, Torrie continued to the far back corner of the club. She was working off the premise of life imitating art. Check out any spy movie or gangster flick, and the club owner always runs his business out of a private room in the back. Masterson proved no different. Torrie saw two old friends standing guard outside a small doorway with a glass-and-silver-beaded curtain. Not bothering to play the games she had played outside, Torrie strolled right up to the thugs, looked them each in the eyes, and said, "Please tell Mister Masterson that there's a friend waiting to see him."

"Didn't expect you to stop by tonight," the thug with the crew cut said. She had mentally nicknamed him Thug One though she didn't bother to share that title with him.

"Was afraid Mister Masterson may have changed his mind about you," said the man of a dozen silver pieces. Naturally, he was now Thug Two.

Torrie leaned forward, getting up on her toes to speak clearly into both of their ears over the pounding beat of the dated techno. "The night is still young, boys. I'm not quite sure I've made up my own mind yet."

The effect was not lost on either thug. Thug One pulled his jacket closed before turning to step through the beaded curtain. Torrie flashed Thug Two a smile while she waited. She could tell her dress was having the same effect on him as it was his friend. Or more specifically, the contents of the dress were.

"Right this way," Thug One said as he returned. He held the curtain aside and Torrie walked in, brushing her hand over his crew cut and throwing a wink back at the other guard. It never hurt to flirt with the bodyguards. Making friends with them could ultimately come in handy.

Torrie was ushered into a room that would have done any movie villain proud. *Intimate* would have been the proper word for this atmosphere. Anywhere else, it would be *tiny*. A single table sat surrounded by a booth upholstered in silver-tone leather. Dietrich Masterson sat in the middle of that booth, head-to-head with a man Torrie thought she vaguely recognized as some real estate mogul. They looked to be finishing up business, because she clearly got the vibe that the man was being dismissed. It was also clear that the man didn't like having to make an abrupt departure. Torrie could tell by the way he sneered at her when he left. She didn't usually get that reaction outside the ring.

"I hope I'm not interrupting anything," Torrie said as she slid into the booth. It was much quieter back here, away from the noise of the club.

"Not at all," Masterson said as he leaned in for a hello kiss. "But I must say this is a pleasant surprise."

"I heard you mention you'd be here last night," Torrie said. "I figured it might be fun to stop by. You know, considering how I had to leave so early this morning."

"It was disappointing to wake up this morning alone with nothing but my pillow for company," he said.

"Well, I couldn't stay out all night," she said. "My little puppy doesn't like to be left alone for too long."

"I understand," Masterson said. "I don't like to be left alone either."

Torrie wasn't sure if he was serious or just playing along. She knew it was a risk just disappearing on him like she had, but she wasn't about to wake up in bed beside him. True, nothing had happened, but he didn't have to know that. If she had stayed, he might have wanted a repeat performance of what she hadn't done the night before. And there were only so many things that Torrie would do for her country.

After she had downloaded the useless information from his computer, she carried him to his bedroom, stripped him down, and left him there to sleep off the drug she had slipped in his drink. She figured a man like Masterson would never admit to having forgotten spending a night of passion with a woman like her. He wouldn't even admit it to himself. And so long as he *thought* that they had slept together, Torrie wasn't going to be quick to let him think otherwise. Over her lifetime, people had made much worse assumptions about her.

Before he could pursue the subject of her abrupt departure, a waitress came through the beaded curtain.

"Something to drink?" Masterson asked Torrie.

"Whatever you want," Torrie said, leaving her meaning up to interpretation.

"Bring a bottle of the 'ninety Dom," Masterson said.

The waitress raised her eyebrows and glanced in Torrie's direction. If he was trying to impress her with his order, he was wasting his time. She preferred slamming back beers with the boys. Of course, Torrie wasn't about to let him know that, so she snuggled up closer to show him how much she appreciated the order.

Masterson certainly didn't mind the close contact and threw an arm around her, holding her closer. This was working even better than Torrie had hoped. She was only inches away from her ultimate objective: his cell phone.

chapter
eighteen

Batista watched as the last barrel was stacked beside the security booth. The annex building had been cleared of everything except the empty barrels waiting to be filled with the next load of crap. The move was going a lot faster than he had anticipated, which was a good thing. He could give the guys a couple hours to rest in the back before the trucks arrived and then go about his business with less people around. This undercover stuff was easier than he had expected . . . so long as nobody asked him to go skulking around in underground tunnels anymore.

Aboveground, things had been going so smoothly that he almost forgot he was in the middle of an illicit operation. In fact, the only thing that was bothering him at the moment was the old guy working the fork-lift, who kept staring at him. After the guy put down the last barrel and parked the forklift off to the side, Batista figured it was time to ask about it. The last thing he needed was someone watching him when he did what had to be done next.

Batista joined the six guys he had been working with all night moving the barrels. "Good job, guys," he said. "You can all cut out for a few hours. Grab a few winks in the back. I'll come get you when it's time to work again."

"Thanks, man," Frank said. He seemed to be the spokesman for the group. He had been the first to welcome Batista, and was quick to offer suggestions for the new guy. The others kept their distance. He wasn't sure if they were intimidated or they just all wanted his job. Either way, he wanted them out of the way so he could talk with Charlie, the guy that was still openly gawking at him.

"Yeah," Batista said. He was a little unnerved by the staring and couldn't take his own eyes off Charlie in return. "You can all go in back . . . Whenever you want . . . Now would be good."

"Hey, Charlie, what's with the moony eyes?"

Frank asked. Apparently Batista wasn't the only one that had noticed. "Stop staring at the new guy. I think you're freaking him out."

"Sorry," Charlie mumbled. "It's just uncanny."

"What is?" Batista asked.

"You look just like him."

Oh, shit.

"Who's he look like?" Frank asked.

"That wrestler," Charlie said. "The one that thinks he's a movie star now. What's his name? That Rock guy."

Batista let out the breath he wasn't aware he had been holding. He didn't know whether to be relieved or offended. He looked *nothing* like that Hollywood pretty boy.

For the first time in the evening, all the guys laughed.

"Man, what would The Rock be doing out here?" Frank was laughing louder than them all.

"Get the hell out of here," Batista said, joking along with them. He received several pats on the back for being a good sport as the guys went to the break room. Now that they were out of the way, there were only a couple guys still hanging around. Batista checked out the stacks of barrels and confirmed that they had been well placed to block all angles of the security cameras around the room. Batista allowed himself a smile as he started inspecting the stacks. Even if Ray *was* watching from the security booth, Batista wouldn't have looked the least bit suspicious. He was just doing his job.

Once Batista was safely behind the dangerous barrels, he slipped in between the rows and squatted down on the floor against the wall to the security booth. He took the mini-screwdriver out of his back pocket and began removing the screws from the connector box. It only took a few seconds to give him access to the system. Once it was open, all he had to do was attach the transmitter to a couple wires, then close the panel back up. He was back out of the rows of barrels in under a minute. But his work wasn't quite over yet.

Chavo closed out of Hunter's laptop. He had gotten everything he could from it. He had done everything he could do *with* it. The aptly titled lockbox file was still securely locked. Considering there was a full night of prep ahead of them, there would be plenty of opportunities to get Fischer's laptop off his desk. The problem was that Chavo couldn't be sure how long it would take to break into the file. It wasn't something that he could attempt during a simple bathroom break. Add to that the fact that he'd have to do it all under the watchful eyes of the security guy, and it presented a nice little challenge for him. But one thing Chavo Guerrero liked both in the ring and in life was a challenge.

And now, he decided, it was time to move.

Chavo left Hunter's office to find Batista. It wasn't exactly a difficult thing to do, considering the place was a lot emptier than the last time he had stepped out of the office. It looked like they had finished moving the barrels to the staging area. That was a good thing. It meant that Batista was ready for the next phase of the plan.

With the laptop under his arm, Chavo nodded to Batista and continued on to Fischer's office. He could feel Batista watching him as he walked. They'd have to time this perfectly.

"How's it going, Mister Fischer?" Chavo asked from the boss's doorway. He made sure to keep half of his body behind the doorframe to hide the laptop.

"Going well," Fischer said. "Chad, is it?"

Chavo had to think for a moment. "Chuck," he said quickly. Batista was Brad. He was Chuck. *Thank God Hunter wasn't around to witness that.*

"What's it look like out there?" Fischer said.

"Pretty good," Chavo said. "Why don't you come check it out?"

"That's okay," Fischer said. "The men work better when I'm not hovering around them."

"Good point," Chavo said as he looked out into the warehouse. His eyes met with Batista's, and he gave his partner a nod. Batista nodded back and then went over to the annex.

"Well, I'll be getting back to work," Chavo said. "But first, I wanted to thank you. Things have been tough for me lately, and this job has really come along at the right time."

"I'm glad I could help," Fischer said with a level of smugness that negated any compassion in his words. "You stick around after tonight, and I promise you there won't be any more hard times for you. This business is taking off, and there are plenty of opportunities for you to get in on the ground floor."

"Thanks, Mister Fischer. That means—"

The sound of crashing metal cut him off.

"OH, SHIT!" someone yelled. "Watch out."

Chavo's eyes went wide as he turned to see what was going on in the warehouse. A stack of barrels had fallen and were rolling across the warehouse floor toward the lab. Ray had just burst out of the security booth and was running toward the barrels in a vain attempt to stop them. Then Fischer blew past Chavo, running toward the commotion faster than Chavo thought the guy could move.

Chavo moved just as quickly, dashing into Fischer's

office, swiping the laptop off the desk and replacing it with Hunter's. So long as no one opened it up, they wouldn't notice the difference. Chavo was out of the office with the laptop in the time it took the situation in the warehouse to settle down. His eyes met Batista's, and he gave his partner a nod to confirm "mission accomplished."

"It's okay," Batista yelled to the group of men running from the barrels as they hit the opposite wall. "They're empties. The forklift must have dinged the stack earlier. They just lost their balance and fell. Sorry, Mister Fischer."

"That's okay, Buck," Fischer said, getting Batista's cover name totally wrong.

Batista shrugged off the mistake. "But while you're here, I got a couple questions."

Chavo left Batista to distract the boss while he returned to Hunter's office. He plugged the NSA's hacking device into the computer port and went to work, bringing up the lockbox icon. From there it was a simple matter of waiting for the NSA device to run through the possible passwords that would reveal the hidden information. Chavo suspected that a guy like Fischer probably kept his password written on a piece of paper taped under the desk blotter or something like that, but he didn't want to risk getting caught sneaking back into the office to look. It didn't matter, since the hacking device only took a moment to open the file.

Success!

Chavo was about to start downloading the file when he realized that he didn't have to. The file didn't contain anything that the NSA could use in their case. It did, however, include information that would be necessary to ensure the success of this mission and minimize the loss of life.

The lockbox file wasn't a file at all. It was a triggering device that would wipe out any and all evidence of the illegal meth lab operation. But this didn't just purge the computer files. The trigger was linked to an explosive device somewhere on the premises that would take out all physical evidence . . . including every person in the place.

Chavo froze for what felt like a minute, but was probably only a few seconds. He had to find a way to disable the trigger. If Fischer set the timer on the bomb when the raid started, there wasn't going to be much of a chance to stop it then. Considering all the illegal chemicals and toxic barrels in the place, Chavo wasn't just worried for his own life or the lives of the NSA agents or even his coworkers. If the bomb went off, it would send out a poisonous cloud that would do more damage to Brooklyn than most dirty bombs a terrorist could smuggle into the country. He needed to find a way to get Batista to stall Fischer a while longer. This work was going to take more time than he anticipated.

Unfortunately, time was something that had just run out.

"Now, what is it you think you're doing with *that?*" Ray asked as he stood blocking the doorway.

chapter
nineteen

The waitress came back into the room, leaning the ice bucket against her hip to keep it from tipping. She placed the ice bucket beside the table nearest Masterson. The girl ran through a rather ornate and totally needless show of preparing the glasses and bottle for them. When she finally got around to opening the bottle, Torrie didn't even hear the hint of a pop in the quiet room. The show continued as the waitress poured a little into each glass. Then a little more. This was the longest that Torrie had ever waited for a drink in her life. Finally, the waitress handed them their glasses and backed out of the room like a proper servant.

"To three nights in a row," Masterson said as he toasted with his champagne.

"Or more," Torrie added as she raised her glass and took a sip. The champagne slipped between her lips and into her mouth, where it danced across her tongue and down her throat. She had never understood the big deal people made over expensive drinks until that moment. There was something about the taste and the texture that was unlike anything she had ever put in her mouth. The burst of flavor remained on her tongue long after the drink sank into her body.

"Well?" Masterson asked before she was fully over the experience.

She wasn't surprised that his ego required a little more stroking. "Delicious," she said, and meant it.

"Just like you." He leaned in for a kiss. Torrie shivered as their lips touched.

"Sorry," she said as she pulled away from him.

"Never had that reaction before," he said with a smile.

"It's a little chilly in here." She added a fake shiver to emphasize the point.

"Yes, we keep it cool for the drinks," Masterson said. "Champagne should be served at around forty-five degrees Fahrenheit. Since most of our clientele can't be bothered to wait the fifteen minutes it takes to properly chill a bottle, we make sure our reserves are rotated through the refrigerators as the night progresses so they are always at perfect temperature. But from the moment champagne is poured from the bottle, it starts moving to room temperature. Keeping it cool in here enhances the experience even more for my guests."

Torrie didn't really care for the lesson in champagne storage and proper drinking habits. She had other things in mind at the moment. "I see," she said, feigning interest. "But what's good for the champagne isn't so good for the girl in the thin silk dress."

"Here," Masterson said as he took off his jacket. "Allow me." He draped the jacket over Torrie's shoulders. She immediately snuggled up inside its warm interior, feeling the weight of his phone on the inside pocket. "How's that?" he asked.

"Perfect," she replied as she pulled the jacket tightly around her. As she raised her glass with her left hand, her right hand was busy inside pulling the phone out of the pocket. She continued her work as they exchanged small talk. They both told lies about their jobs while Torrie popped open her handy little NSA compact. This time she felt for the smaller of the two connectors and attached it to Masterson's phone.

Considering how he had reacted the night before when she tried to play keep-away, Torrie suspected that it was more than just a phone. From the little she had the chance to see while she played with it, she knew the phone had impressive PDA capabilities. She thought it was quite likely that the phone had the all-important information on Masterson's business dealings saved inside. It made sense that he would keep that information on him at all times.

Once the download was complete, the compact gently vibrated in her hand to alert her that the job was done. She disconnected the device and slipped it back in the pocket. This was done not a moment too soon, as the phone rang as soon as it fell into place.

Torrie covered her relief as she reached into the pocket and handed the phone over to him. "I was wondering when that was going to interrupt," she said.

"Sorry," he apologized for the hundredth time in their short relationship.

"I'll be right back," she said as she slid out of his jacket and the booth. He just smiled and took his call.

Torrie left the small room, only pausing to ask the guards where the ladies' room was located. They directed her with a grunt to the side. She already knew the destination. Mister McMahon had provided her with a layout of the place while she prepped for the mission. The ladies' room was conveniently located along the corridor by the champagne storage and the back door. She continued past the growing crowd, disappointed to see that her "friends" from outside had managed to make their way in. The three girls were loudly toasting to a "Night of Wickedness" and chugging down their dainty drinks. Torrie supposed that they had just come from a certain Broadway show and figured they thought they were having a cool New York experience. Conveniently for the Jersey girls, the desperate guys around them were eating it up.

Torrie brushed past the women, heading for the ladies' room and beyond. Once she was alone in the tight hallway, she continued to the back door, where she was greeted by the warning that an alarm would sound if she opened it. This was not a problem for Torrie. She reached into her purse, pulled out another one of the NSA's convenient little devices, attached it to the door, pushed it open, and enjoyed the silence.

Torrie would have preferred to go out the front door, but she knew the guards would be watching and wondering what she was doing leaving the boss so quickly after they'd just got their drinks. Then there would be the chauffeur to get past once she was outside. It was much easier to ditch out the back and disappear into the night.

Considering a dark alley on a Friday night was no

place for a lady, Torrie reached into her purse and took out the NSA keychain she had been issued when she completed her training. This would have to do in lieu of a gun as she made her way out to the next street. She was especially glad she had it when she heard the club door open behind her and turned to see Masterson's two guards coming out.

"You missed the bathroom, lady," Thug One said.

"That's okay," Torrie replied. "I know a cleaner one down the street."

"Mister Masterson don't like it when his dates skip out on him," said Thug Two.

"Oh," Torrie replied as they got closer. "Does that happen often?"

She didn't bother to wait for a reply. She held the keychain out in front of her and pressed on the controller. The thug with all the silver on barely had time to laugh at the toy before it came to life, shocking the hell out of him and dropping him to the ground. Torrie briefly wondered if all that metal may have amplified the shock. It was an interesting question for a later time.

Thug One quickly swung into action. He kicked out his leg, catching Torrie's hand and ripping the keychain from her grasp. Without missing a beat, he swung a fist at her. Torrie moved quickly, ducking the blow and coming up with an uppercut of her own, getting him squarely on the jaw. She had come up against bigger opponents than him before.

Torrie backed up to give herself some room, slipped off her heels, and waited. Taking off her shoes wasn't the wisest thing to do in a filthy alley, but she preferred to fight barefoot. Heels were not conducive to a strong defense.

Once the guy regained his footing, he came at her. Torrie surprised him with a dropkick that sent him to the ground. Hard. She then dropped with an elbow to his face.

But the thug wasn't out of it yet. He reached up and grabbed her arm, pulling her down to the ground. Torrie countered quickly, rolling on top of him and hitting him with a barrage of fists to the chest. The big man absorbed the punches and threw her off him.

Torrie landed across the alley, but bounced right back up. The thug was slower to rise, and Torrie charged him with a knee to the face. That turned out to be her finisher, as the thug dropped back to the ground and didn't get up. Torrie only wished her dog Chloe was there so she could give the thug the Tush Push just to add insult to his injury.

Torrie's chest was heaving as she rose off the ground, trying to catch her breath. Her green dress was a shambles. It was not intended for rolling around dirty alleys in. The slit had ripped all the way up her thigh, and her breasts were nearly bursting out of the torn bodice. But the two guys laid flat out before her were certainly worth the cost of one dress. Besides, she could probably invoice the cost to the NSA, since the dress had been lost in battle.

Torrie picked up her purse, which had dropped during the fight. She checked to confirm that the compact was still safe inside. The night would have been a total success, if it weren't for the jolting shock from her NSA stun-gun keychain as it was used against her. When Torrie dropped to the ground, the last thing she saw above her was Dietrich Masterson holding that powerful mini-weapon.

chapter
twenty

Hunter pulled up to the security gate at the Port of Newark and drove right through, even though it was long past regular business hours. The guard didn't even bother to look up from his newspaper. This was the kind of lax port security the media was always hyped up about. *Just goes to prove that no matter who owns the ports, anything can get through when the right amount of money changes hands,* Hunter thought.

It wasn't hard to find Fischer's operation. They weren't that far from the entrance that Hunter had come across at the third stack of shipping containers.

At first, Hunter was worried that he didn't see any of the NSA's men, but then he realized that was the point. He knew that Thompson and his people were all there keeping watch and recording the event for posterity and prosecution.

Hunter pulled his SUV up along where the forklifts were carefully loading the trucks. It only took him a minute to find Trent. The nagging suspicion hadn't left Hunter. *Why did Trent say he didn't know anything about Masterson?* But there was nothing Hunter could do about it at the moment. He just had to let the night play out and see where it took him. He wished he could find Thompson and warn him that something else might be going down, but he knew he couldn't risk it. The WWE crew may have been doing the loading, but the truck drivers were on Fischer's payroll. Anything out of the ordinary could lose them the shipment. He was sure there were contingency plans in place to keep the illegal contraband from getting to its destination if things went south.

"Started without me, huh?" he asked as he joined Trent to watch the loading. It was best to leave things alone for the moment and act like nothing was wrong.

"Faster we get in, faster we get out," Trent said nervously. Now all the nervousness seemed like overacting. Hunter didn't know why he'd never seen it before.

"Can't argue with that," Hunter said. "Time estimate?"

"Couple hours."

"We sure no one's going to stumble across us here? It's not like all these trucks and workers aren't noticeable," Hunter said.

"You know Fischer," Trent said. "Anyone that could cause problems has been neatly paid off. We're covered. And I'm sure your guys have alerted the locals to keep away from the area too."

"We should have a clear shot from here to the warehouse," Hunter said.

Trent relaxed visibly. "Good."

"I'll go check on the men," Hunter said.

"Sounds like a plan," Trent replied, sounding calm for the first time since Triple H had met him. That alone made Hunter nervous.

Hunter walked over to the men loading the boxes onto the trucks. Even though he had been working with many of them for years, he acted like they had all just met recently. The truck drivers were all keeping watch over the loading, and every one of them looked ready to bolt if things got suspicious. One of the roadies stood out to Hunter over the rest. That was largely because this particular roadie wasn't a roadie at all. John Cena had been slipped into the group in case Hunter needed backup at the scene. It seemed like an unnecessary precaution earlier, especially considering how Hunter and Cena didn't have the best of relationships at the moment. But now that Trent was under suspicion of some darker motivation, Cena was a welcome addition to the team.

At least, that's what Hunter hoped.

The load-in continued as planned. The time-consuming part came from the fact that the containers bringing in the chemicals were not kept in the same part of the yard. To avoid detection, they had been shipped under three different front companies and stored on separate sections of the ship. After they were offloaded, they were also stacked in different places in the yards. The fact that only a small selection of all containers are subjected to search when they come into port made it easier to grease the right palms to avoid these three as long as they didn't come in together.

Fischer had provided detailed instructions on the exact reference numbers and locations of the containers. Unfortunately two of the three had been unloaded in the middle of the stacks of containers, and a crane was required to get the cargo to ground level for transfer. Hunter was surprised that all the commotion was going on unnoticed in the middle of the night, but he figured that was the kind of protection a man like Dietrich Masterson provided for Fischer. There was no way Fischer could have done this on his own.

But that still didn't explain what this operation was giving Masterson. It seemed too small for the man, considering his other criminal interests. And Trent wasn't giving any clue to what else could be going on. Hunter considered checking out some of the boxes to see if they indeed were chemical shipments, but he couldn't think of a way to do it without putting anyone on alert. Besides, he knew the trucks would be under surveillance from the moment they left the dockyards. Even if Masterson had slipped a little something extra into the shipment, the NSA would have the trucks tagged. If one of the trucks went astray, it was all the better for them. It could lead directly back to Masterson.

But if Trent is involved, he won't let that happen. As far as Hunter was concerned, this new wrinkle was making less and less sense to him. Maybe he was just being overly suspicious. There could be a perfectly logical reason why Trent had acted like he never saw Masterson before. The guy was nervous to begin with. Maybe Dietrich Masterson just made him more nervous. So nervous that Trent was afraid to go against the crime lord.

No. Hunter still wasn't buying it. Something was up.

It was nearing morning by the time the five trucks were fully loaded with the illegal chemicals. The drivers had suggested sending each truck out as it was loaded so they would be less noticeable. Five trucks tooling through Brooklyn in the wee hours of the morning weren't exactly unobtrusive. But Hunter and Trent overruled the decision, knowing that it would be easier for the NSA to keep track of them together. Besides, Hunter didn't want to risk any of the toxic waste getting loaded and out of the warehouse before the NSA could move in.

"That it, boss?" Cena asked for show as they closed the last truck.

"Looks like it," Hunter said as he and Trent exchanged looks. "Time to head 'em up and move 'em out."

The five truck drivers didn't bother to cover their looks of annoyance at having to stick around for so long. They each took to the wheel of their respective trucks and started the engines. Hunter sent home the WWE roadies so they wouldn't get mixed up in this any more than they already had been. The plan called for Trent to lead the procession and Hunter to bring up the rear to make sure none of the trucks went rogue.

"I'm going to finish things up here," Trent said once the trucks were lined up and ready to leave.

"I've got a few more payouts to make to be sure everyone stays quiet."

"Sounds good," Hunter lied. He was fairly certain this wasn't part of the plan. So far as he knew, all payments had been made up front—at least, that's what Fischer had led him to believe. Besides, what was the point in paying anyone else off if the NSA was about to close down the entire operation?

Hunter suspected that one of two things could be happening. On the purely innocent side, Trent could simply be taking the opportunity to bolt. Technically, with the stuff Chavo had gotten off the servers, it wasn't entirely necessary for Trent to stick around and bear witness for the prosecution. Trent could sneak away and disappear if he didn't have the balls to testify. Of course, the other option was that Trent and Masterson had something else going on at the moment. That worried Hunter more than anything.

Either way, Hunter wasn't about to lose the guy while on the Superstars' watch. Cena, who was still sticking around, looked equally suspicious of the change in plan. A silent look passed between the two Superstars that told Hunter they were both on the same wavelength.

"Meet you back at the warehouse," Hunter said to Trent as he boarded his SUV. "Need a ride?" he asked Cena.

Cena nodded and got in the passenger side.

Hunter took off, but as soon as he turned the corner, he slowed the vehicle. "Meet you back here in five minutes,"

"See you," Cena said as he slipped out of the moving SUV.

Hunter continued after the trucks, past the cargo containers, and to the exit. He could see Trent watching him as soon as he cleared the container units. Once he was off the dock, Hunter pulled over and left the SUV, not wanting to tip off Trent to his return. There was definitely something off about Trent's decision to stay behind.

chapter
twenty-one

The first thing Torrie was aware of was the sound. There was none. No street noise. No traffic. No pulsing beat from the club behind her. Nothing but deadly silence. But that wasn't too much of a surprise, because the next thing she was aware of was the fact that she wasn't lying in an alleyway anymore. The soft cushion beneath her told her that much, but little else. Her mind was still having trouble focusing. She wasn't quite sure what had happened. The last thing she remembered was Dietrich Masterson standing over her.

Torrie tried to open her eyes, but was having a

difficult time. This grogginess wasn't entirely new to her. Having been knocked out before by some of her Diva enemies, she was regretfully familiar with the sensation. This was different somehow. There was something lingering around the edges of her consciousness that she had never experienced before.

Finally, she was able to open her eyes slightly. Through those bleary slits, Torrie was able to make out the fact that she was lying on a bed. By the cold design of the room, she figured she must be in Masterson's apartment. A guest room, probably, since she had visited the master bedroom briefly on her last visit. A dim light was coming in through the windows. It was morning already. *That can't be right.*

Her movement was limited. She felt constrained, and it took a moment for it to register that her arms and feet were bound to the bed. It wasn't necessarily the first time she had found herself tied up in bed, but it was certainly the first time it had happened without her consent.

A quick check of the room confirmed that she was alone. Considering how much strength it was taking just to keep her eyes open, Torrie gave in and let them slip shut again. She was safe for the moment and needed to regain her faculties. It was all she could do not to pass out again.

NSA training had included an unfortunate day when Torrie was subjected to the effects of her stungun, so she knew the full strength of the weapon she was wielding. That day was nothing like this. The quick jolt to the senses had knocked her legs out from under her and sent her to the ground quickly, blacking out the world around her. But the effects were not long-lasting. It certainly didn't keep her out a long enough time to transfer her into Masterson's limo, get her up to his apartment, and tie her to his bed, much less keep her out until early morning. No. Something else had obviously been used on her once she was out—something that was still affecting her.

Torrie tried to clear her mind. She tried to focus her thoughts. She was trapped in Masterson's apartment with no way to get in contact with anyone. The NSA hadn't even sanctioned this mission. They certainly weren't about to mount a rescue. Even though she had her WWE partners, Torrie suspected she was entirely on her own. They had other responsibilities this morning. Ones that superseded her being tied to some rich guy's bed.

In pop culture terms, she was about to be disavowed.

The haze was beginning to lift, but Torrie suspected that she might have nodded off briefly, because when she opened her eyes again she was surprised to find Masterson sitting at the foot of the bed. This time her eyes popped open, and she was able to focus. Yet there was still a lingering oddness about her. She didn't quite feel herself.

"Good morning," Masterson said with a plastered-on smile.

"I didn't realize you were into kinky games," Torrie said as she pulled on her constraints. Now that she saw her binds, she realized they were silk scarves. Romantic, yes, but not quite practical in her opinion. "I should tell you, I'm not that kind of girl."

"Really, Larkin, if that in fact is your name," Masterson said, "what kind of girl are you?"

"The kind that will be calling the police if you don't untie me right this second," Torrie said.

He laughed. "I don't think so. You won't be getting untied. You won't be calling the police."

"Listen, freak, I don't know who you think you are . . ."

"Don't you?" Masterson asked. "No. I think you know exactly who I am. I think you know what I do. And I think you were trying to get proof of those things."

"I don't know what you're talking about."

"I'm talking about your little metal toy." He was obviously referring to the compact she had used to steal the information off his PDA. Torrie wasn't surprised that he had found it. He wouldn't have taken her to his place and tied her up without doing a little search of her belongings. "Now, who do you work for?"

"Whatever," Torrie said, turning away from him.

She heard Masterson get up from his chair. A moment later she felt his hand slide across her chin. Then her head was suddenly yanked to the side. He was forcing her to look at him. "I said, who are you working for?"

Torrie's mind flashed to the answer and before she realized she was saying anything, the words were tumbling out of her mouth. "Mister McMahon."

"McMahon?" Masterson asked. "That doesn't do me any good. What's the name of your organization?"

Again, Torrie tried to ignore him, but she could not stop herself. It was suddenly clear that she had not only been slipped a sedative, but she was on some kind of truth serum as well. "The WWE."

"WWE? Is that a branch of the FBI? CIA? What is this organization?"

"World Wrestling Entertainment."

Masterson laughed again. This time there was actual humor in the laugh. "Cute. I like that. So you're a lady wrestler."

"I'm a *Diva*," she said proudly, figuring she'd just go with the flow. In this case, the truth didn't really hurt at all. He'd never believe it.

"That you are," Masterson said. "I've obviously underestimated your training if you withstand the drugs I've given you. No worries. I just need to make a phone call, and I can get someone over here that is well practiced at getting information from unwilling subjects."

Torrie didn't like the sound of that. But trying to play Masterson while she was on some truth-serum-type drug seemed too dangerous. She needed to find a way out of there or give her mind some more time to clear first. So Torrie stayed silent as she watched Masterson leave the room.

As soon as the door shut behind him, Torrie was working at her binds. The silk scarves shouldn't be too hard to get out of, even though the limited movements were already burning her skin. Torrie decided to focus her attention on her right wrist, as that seemed to be the scarf with the most amount of slack. But before she could really get to work, she heard a commotion in the outer room. It sounded like a fight.

A very brief fight.

Within moments, the door to her room reopened, and Masterson's chauffeur stepped inside. It was the first time she had seen the man from the front, and she was surprised by how familiar he looked. She was even more surprised when he took off his chauffeur hat and his hair came right off with it, revealing the beautiful bald head of Stone Cold Steve Austin.

chapter
twenty-two

It took Hunter a few minutes to double back and catch up with Cena. The Port of Newark wasn't exactly a small place. In fact, once they were back together and tracking Trent together, it was still unclear where he was going. But that uncertainty only lasted a short time. The noise from ahead indicated they were nearing their destination.

It sounded like heavy machinery. Considering the port was supposed to be closed over the weekend, there sure was a lot of activity going on. Hunter figured that was the explanation right there. The idea struck him like a double-arm DDT from Mick Foley.

Trent had set up Fischer with the NSA as a diversion. They had been so busy loading Fischer's shipment by the front entrance that nobody would notice what was going on at the ass end of the place—especially if the heavy lifting was held off until the truck caravan led the NSA away from the dockyard. It only took him the turn of one corner for him to confirm his suspicion. A crane was busy lifting cargo containers and loading them onto a train.

Trent continued on toward the commotion and greeted the pair of big guys that Hunter recognized from the other day, Masterson's bodyguards. They both looked like they were ready for action, even though the white guy with the crew cut looked like he had already been through the ringer recently. Hunter and Cena positioned themselves behind a stack of crates off to the side so they could avoid being seen.

"Another shipment of chemicals?" Cena guessed.

"Doubt it," Hunter said. "No reason to be all sneaky about it if it's just more of the same."

"What do you think it is?"

"Don't know," Hunter said. "But I'm more interested to know what Trent has to do with all this. He was the one that brought the NSA into this deal."

"You think he's working for Masterson?"

"Seems like a good way to get something special

into the country," Hunter said. "Get the NSA interested in Fischer's drugs. Have the government boys arrange it with the Port Authority to keep clear of the area so they can track it. Then Masterson slips in something much more dangerous right under everyone's noses while his partner goes down on the meth charge."

"We should call Thompson," Cena said.

"Can't," Hunter replied. "Communication blackout."

Hunter was pissed. He didn't like being played. Trent had used him—and even worse, made him feel sorry for the snitch. Hunter had even worried about the guy and his fake little nervous condition. But Trent wasn't a snitch. In fact, he was in it deeper than the actual criminal Hunter was first sent to take down. *Good job knowing your enemy, Director Thompson,* Hunter thought.

"We need to find out what's in those containers," Hunter said as he went on the move.

Hunter and Cena did their best to stay behind the containers as they approached the train. It wasn't an easy walk. There were at least two dozen men working on loading the containers and guarding the train. This was a much more impressive operation than Fischer's rinky-dink little chemical score. Every single one of Masterson's men looked like they easily belonged in a wrestling ring. Hunter and Cena were easily outnumbered. They had to be extremely careful.

When they reached the last stack of containers, there was about a fifty-foot gap before the train. With so many people in the area, they were going to have to time it just right. Hunter thought about trying to find a way to cause a distraction, but there was nothing in the vicinity that could help him with that. He was just going to have to rely on luck.

Hunter watched and waited as the forklift finished loading another container onto the train. The act of attaching it to the platform seemed to take attention from just about everyone in the vicinity. It was now or never.

"Go," he whispered to Cena, and they both dashed to the train, slipping in between cars. They stopped and waited for the yelling to begin, but nothing happened. They were in the clear. Hunter climbed up the ladder and pushed on the door. It opened, allowing Hunter to enter with Cena coming up behind him.

It was dark in the container. Hunter didn't want to close the door behind them, but he had to. An open door would be an invitation for someone to investigate. Since Hunter didn't have a flashlight or a lighter or even a match on him, he used the only source of light he could find: the screen of his cell phone. He felt like an aging hippie at a rock concert as the pale blue light illuminated the interior of the container. Stacks of crates ran from floor to ceiling around them. The shortest and stockiest of those crates sat alone on the far end of the container. The Superstars walked toward it. Cena tried to lift the lid, but it was sealed tight.

"Any ideas?" Hunter asked.

Cena responded by sending his fist crashing through the top of the wooden crate.

"Any *quieter* ideas?" Hunter asked through clenched teeth.

The damage done, they waited to see if anyone came in after the noise. When no one did, Cena used his newly created handle to get leverage on the crate and pull the top off. The metal nails whined as the wood separated. Cena dropped the splintered wood to the floor beside the crate. Hunter held his phone over the crate, and the two men peered inside. Even though his mind had expected the worst, Hunter was still surprised by what he saw: a huge stack of semi-automatic machine guns. And that was just the one crate. No telling what kinds of weapons were in all the other boxes and all the other containers.

"We need to get Thompson back here," Cena said as he lifted one of the guns out of the crate. Hunter held up the cell phone as Cena pulled the clip. It was empty, unsurprisingly. Shipping loaded guns was not exactly wise.

Hunter pushed number 1 on his cell phone, figuring he could screw the communications blackout. The problem was, there was no way to tell Thompson to do that on the other end. The NSA director refused to answer the call. Hunter left a message but figured it wasn't going to be heard until after the mission. And that could be too late.

With no other NSA contact programmed into his phone, Hunter dialed his only other option: Vince. Hunter just hoped that the chairman would answer his phone at the early hour. There was no need to worry, however. Vince picked up on the first ring.

Considering that they were safely closed into the container, Hunter put Vince on speakerphone and quickly filled him in on the situation.

"How many men?" Vince asked.

"Too many," Hunter said. He knew that he and Cena could take out most of the group, but not everyone. Especially considering some of them had guns that he was pretty sure were actually loaded.

"Mister McMahon, this might be the time to reevaluate your policy on our use of guns in our work," Cena added.

"Nothing we can do about that now," Vince said. "Unless you think you can use anything around you."

"I don't think we can keep breaking into crates to look for ammunition and stay hidden long," Hunter said. "We need backup, and I can't call in Chavo and Batista because they're in that damn warehouse."

"I'll see what I can do," Vince said. "You two keep an eye on the situation. And don't do anything unless you have to."

Vince cut off the call, leaving Hunter and Cena alone in the dark container.

"We need to get better cover," Hunter said. "And see what we can do to slow things down. This train can't leave the yard."

chapter
twenty-three

Torrie rubbed at her wrists. They were red and sore and still burned a little from the silk scarves. She took great pleasure in watching Steve use those same scarves to tie Masterson's hands behind his back. She took even greater pleasure in the goose egg on Masterson's head that was the cause of his current unconscious state.

"What are you doing here, Steve?" Torrie asked as he finished up. Austin had supposedly been resting up in Texas for the past month because he had aggravated his old neck injury.

"Long-term undercover assignment," Austin said. "Thompson needed someone who could go in as a driver and bodyguard for Masterson. He pulled me in a few weeks ago."

"That's why he didn't want us involved in this," Torrie guessed.

Stone Cold nodded. "He didn't want to risk my mission. No one knows I'm in deep 'cept him and me." Suddenly, Phil Thompson didn't seem like the total ass that Torrie had taken him for. "He needed someone to slowly gain Masterson's trust," Austin continued. "I was getting there, too, till you had to go and get all up in things and get to him faster than I ever could."

Torrie flushed with pride in herself. Even though she had gotten captured, she had managed to get access to Masterson's files pretty fast. At least, she hoped that she had. "Did you see a small metal compact that's not really a compact?" she asked. "Masterson took it from me."

"In his office," Austin said. He must have seen Torrie look down at the unconscious Masterson, because he added, "He ain't going nowhere anytime soon."

Torrie was glad to hear that as she and Austin went for Masterson's office. The NSA device was on the guy's desk and attached to his computer via the same port she had used the other night, when she had tried to pull things off that computer. "He must have been trying to see what I got," Torrie said as she looked over the screen. Apparently he had brought everything she downloaded up on the computer. She couldn't make heads or tails of most of it, but it looked like she had hit the motherlode.

Torrie went to take the device off the computer, but Austin stopped her. "Hold it," he said. "If I'm right, I think something's going down tonight. This might tell us what."

"It's a drug shipment coming in through Newark," Torrie said. "We're already on it."

"Not that," Austin said. "Something bigger. Much bigger."

"Oh."

As Austin started pounding on the keyboard to bring up any files he could find, Torrie heard the muffled sound of her cell phone ringing. It was nearby. She looked around the room and saw her purse thrown open on one of the guest chairs. She hurried over and pulled the phone out of her bag. Mister McMahon's name was up on the caller ID.

"Yes, Mister McMahon," she said as she opened the phone.

"Where are you?"

"Masterson's apartment," she said. "It's okay. He's

out cold. I got the information off his phone. We've got it up on his computer and are looking at it right now."

"We?" Mister McMahon asked.

"Steve's here."

"Austin?"

Torrie could hear the shock in McMahon's voice. "Um . . . yes?" This was met with silence. "Mister McMahon?"

"Check this out," Austin said as he swiveled the computer screen to face Torrie. She leaned over and did not like what she saw.

"Mister McMahon," she said into the phone, "the drug shipment's a cover-up."

"I know," he finally replied. "Hunter and Cena are at the port right now, keeping a weapons shipment under surveillance. They can't get through to anyone for help. I need you and Austin to get to the port now."

"Okay," she said.

"Wait a minute," McMahon said. "You've got *all* Masterson's files?"

"So far as we can tell."

"Can you bring up anything on Fischer's warehouse?" McMahon asked. "See if there's a way to get a call in to Chavo and Batista. We're going to need all the backup we can get."

"We'll see," Torrie said. She told Austin what to look for. He tapped a few keys and brought up a file on the warehouse. "There," she said, pointing to a document that said "Specs."

Austin opened the file, and they both quickly scanned the information. There was nothing on the phone system, but there was an intriguing link to a familiar document she had heard about earlier, the one entitled "Lockbox." Torrie pointed it out, and Austin clicked it open. It only took a second for both of them to come to the conclusion that their priorities had just changed.

"Mister McMahon, we have a problem," Torrie said. "It's that lockbox file. It looks like it's some kind of failsafe for the warehouse."

"What kind of failsafe?"

"At the first sign of trouble, Fischer can type a code into his computer and blow the place up to destroy all the evidence."

"And send a toxic cloud into the air that could destroy half of Brooklyn," Vince added. "You've got to get there before the NSA raid."

"But what about Hunter and John?" Torrie asked.

"They're not going to do anything until they have to," Mr. McMahon said. "This takes priority. Get moving." The phone went dead.

"We have to get to Brooklyn," Torrie said.

"Well, I think I know where we can get a car," Austin said with a sly smile.

Torrie disconnected the NSA device and slipped it into her purse. "What about Masterson?"

"We'll take him with us," he said. "Don't want him getting away."

Torrie followed Austin as he went back to the other room and easily threw Masterson over his shoulder as if he was an oversized pillow instead of a full-grown man. Together, they left the apartment without bothering to worry about the security cameras they both knew were placed throughout the building.

Not surprisingly, Austin had already taken Masterson's key off him and used it to call the elevator. It only took a couple seconds for the car to arrive. As they stepped inside, Torrie worried that someone else might stop the elevator on the way down and get on. It would be hard to explain an unconscious body slung over a chauffeur's shoulder. Luckily it was around six o'clock in the morning on a Saturday, so they were able to ride down the entire way without stopping. She doubted they would have the same luck when they hit the lobby. Best-case scenario, they'd have to get by the desk guard. It was unlikely that they'd be able to carry out one of the more prominent residents of the building unconscious and tied up without getting the guards' attention.

Boy, was I wrong, she thought as they met no resistance.

The guard didn't look surprised. In fact, he hardly looked up from his magazine. Austin mumbled something about a rough night and breezed right past the guy. Torrie guessed that he had spent the past month building a relationship with the staff, because the guard didn't even say anything as they went right past him. Their luck continued out on the street, where there was no one around to see Steve load Masterson into the trunk of his town car and peel out.

"You know where we're going?" Austin asked.

"I think so," she replied.

"Well, hold on, because we're going to get from Manhattan to Brooklyn in record time."

Torrie adjusted her seat belt and grabbed hold of the door as the town car weaved through traffic. She was amazed at Austin's skill in working his way through streets. Thankfully it was light Saturday-morning traffic, or she was pretty sure they would have been riding on the sidewalks. Austin barely paid attention to other vehicles, much less street-lights. Car horns blared around them as they flew through the streets of Manhattan. Again, their luck seemed to hold out; they didn't hear a siren at all as they blew through intersection after intersection. Of course, if the police did come after them, Torrie doubted Austin would even slow down. A police escort wouldn't be such a bad thing, considering what they were about to go up against.

On an average day Torrie estimated it would take at least a half hour to get out to the warehouse in Brooklyn. But with Austin driving, she wasn't surprised to find them on the BQE in under ten minutes. She was, however, shocked to find that she had managed to keep what little food she had left in her system down. It was by far the wildest ride she had ever taken in her life.

"There's the warehouse," Torrie said. It looked just as it did in the surveillance photos she had seen during the mission brief, right down to the ramp that led up to the loading bay. "Why are you speeding up?"

"You said they had surveillance cameras outside, right?"

"Yeah."

"So they'll know we're coming."

"I guess."

"Then we don't want to give them the chance to stop us," Steve said as the engine roared. Torrie braced herself as the warehouse loomed in front of her. He was angling the car toward the ramp at the loading dock. She had hoped that he was just going to swing up to the front entrance quickly and then hop out and rush the door. But that didn't seem to be the plan. No. He wasn't planning on stopping by the door. He wasn't planning on stopping at all.

chapter
twenty-four

"What do you want to do?" Batista asked. "Try the old fake-out-the-guard-by-pretending-one-of-us-is-sick routine?"

"That might work," Chavo said. "If there was actually a guard outside. I think everyone's so busy, they've just left us here to rot."

"Mighty kind of them to ignore us," Batista said.

"I was thinking the same thing," Chavo replied. He was almost tempted to laugh at Batista. The big guy had been pacing the room most of the night, which, considering his size, was about three steps before he was forced to turn and walk in the opposite direction. That left very little space for Chavo to get comfortable. He had settled on sitting with his legs crossed on top of Hunter's desk while he considered their options.

"It looks like the only way out is the door." He had already discarded the idea of trying to fit himself through the vent in the back wall. While it was true that he was one of the smaller Superstars, he wasn't that small. There was no way he was going to get out by that route.

After Ray found Chavo working on Fischer's computer, the security chief had shoved Batista into Hunter's office with him and locked them both inside. Since everyone was prepping for the arrival of the illegal chemicals and the transfer out of the toxic waste, there really wasn't much time to interrogate them. Actually, that wasn't true. Ray had wanted to question them immediately. But since both Chavo and Batista were no longer overseeing the workers—and Fischer wouldn't do that himself—the job fell to Ray. This was beyond incompetence in Chavo's mind; ignoring them was the last thing Fischer should be doing after finding two moles in his organization on the same night of a major operation.

But Chavo wasn't about to point that out.

"I think I can get through it," Batista said as he

examined the door. It seemed like your basic flimsy wood door that shouldn't be much of an impediment for someone of Batista's size and bulk. The only problem was deciding what they would do once they were free. They couldn't do anything to risk blowing the NSA's plan. And fighting their way out of the building would certainly interfere with whatever raid was being planned.

But Chavo knew that he couldn't just sit around and wait for the raid to happen either. That lockbox file was too big a risk. With the laptop back in Fischer's office, there was nothing to stop him from triggering the explosive the moment he suspected the raid was going down. All it would take is a signal from Ray when he saw the approaching cars on the outside surveillance, and Fischer could arm the bomb and try to sneak out in the ensuing chaos. Even if Chavo managed to warn the NSA agents about the bomb once they got in, he doubted they'd be able to disarm it in time.

No, the bomb was the bigger problem at the moment. It was far more important to keep that from going off than worrying about losing Fischer before the raid. Of course, the best course of action was to find a way to do both. But considering they were locked in a tiny office, there didn't seem to be a way to get out without causing a commotion.

But when Chavo heard the enormous crash that shook the entire building, he suspected that stealth was no longer a necessity.

"Sounds like our cue," Chavo said.

Batista didn't wait for any further instructions. He stepped as far away from the door as he could get in the small room, then barreled forward. Considering the door opened in, he needed to do more than break the lock. It wasn't a problem, though. The wood splintered around him as he smashed right through.

Chavo hurried out behind him. *Thank God Hunter had Batista store all the toxic chemicals away from the loading dock,* he thought, as there was currently a black town car sticking into the side of the building. Though the choice of entrance was ill advised, it had quite the desired effect.

Workers were scattering in every direction.

Ray was bursting out of the security booth, with his gun leading the way.

Fischer was nowhere to be seen.

And Torrie and Stone Cold Steve Austin were spilling out of the car, looking none the worse for wear.

"What the hell is *he* doing here?" Chavo wondered aloud. But no one had time to answer, because Ray began firing away at the car with his .357 Magnum.

Thankfully, the car had distracted the security chief, and he didn't notice that Chavo and Batista had burst out of their room. Since he was closest, Chavo went for Ray as assorted workers took cover. A quick roundhouse kick knocked the gun from Ray's hand and sent it skittering behind the rows of toxic waste barrels. This seemed to be the sign for half the workers to flee the building, while the more loyal employees joined in on the attack.

As Chavo clashed with Ray, Batista moved toward Torrie and Austin, who were both locked in hand-to-hand combat with a half dozen guys. He pulled Frank off Torrie and was about to fling the guy across the room when he decided on a different course of action. "Get the hell out of here!" he yelled in Frank's face.

No dummy, Frank did exactly as he was told, joining Charlie and a couple other guys as they beat it out of there through the hole in the bay door. Batista knew he should have detained the guys, but quite frankly they were only working stiffs and would probably decide to pursue less hazardous work, all things considered.

The situation didn't seem too bad from his perspective. The lab workers had apparently heard the commotion and were spilling out of the meth lab, their white coats flapping in the wind. None of them were even bothering to stop and join the fight as they blew through the security exit. Their unexcused departure was accompanied by the sound of the klaxon and a flashing red strobe that only added to the commotion. More and more of the staff seemed to be getting away, causing Batista to wonder what the hell Austin and Torrie had been thinking by bursting in like that. There had to be a reason why they would put the mission in jeopardy like that. *And what the hell is Austin even doing here in the first place?* Batista wondered.

But there was no time to get an answer to that particular question.

Before Batista could jump back into the fray, he saw motion out of the corner of his eye. Fischer had finally reappeared. He was running out of his office. The two men locked eyes. Fischer seemed to take in the situation, realizing that there was a lot of trouble between him and the exit. He took off in the opposite direction, heading for the back of the warehouse. Batista started after him, but a nagging suspicion led him to detour into Fischer's office. A quick check on the computer confirmed his worst fear. Fischer had accessed the lockbox file Chavo had mentioned earlier. The screen showed a series of numbers counting down rapidly by the milliseconds.

The warehouse was set to explode in less than ten minutes.

chapter
twenty-five

Batista pounded on the keyboard, but nothing happened. The computer was locked in silent countdown. Since this was Chavo's area of expertise, Batista ran out of the office and back into the battle. Chavo and Ray were locked arm in arm, each trying to get the upper hand. With Ray's back to him, Batista took the opportunity, snuck up behind the guard, and put him in a sleeper hold. Within seconds, Ray lost his grip on Chavo.

"Fischer activated the bomb," Batista said. "I can't stop it."

"I'll see what I can do," Chavo said as he went for the office. "But you need to get Fischer back."

Batista continued to hold onto the struggling Ray until his body started to go limp as he lost consciousness. "Austin, can you take care of this?" Batista asked as he let Ray's body slump to the floor. The guy was only going to be out for a few seconds.

"Got it!" Austin called back as he slammed his last two opponents' heads together, knocking them both out.

That done, Batista ran through the warehouse, heading for the back door. Fischer hadn't even bothered to hide his escape route. The trap door was wide open when Batista reached the storage room. Without pausing to think, he dropped down into the hole and was back in the underground tunnel he thought he had been finished with for good earlier.

The different tunnels branching out around him meant there were several possible directions Fischer could have gone. The obvious choice for Batista was to go the way he and Chavo had taken on their previous trips. At least he knew that led to an exit. But that wouldn't work. Fischer needed to get to an escape vehicle. He had activated a bomb that would release a toxic cloud over the area. He wasn't going to try to leave Brooklyn on foot. And Batista knew the area he and Chavo had come in from had no place to store cars. But that only cut out one of the possible avenues of escape.

Batista took a moment to get his bearings. If he could figure out which tunnel led back to the parking area, he figured, that would probably lead to Fischer. Even though Fischer's own vehicle was regularly parked in front of the warehouse, Batista suspected the guy would have a backup. But then he realized that he was overthinking the situation.

Batista stopped and listened. It was quiet in the tunnel, but that worked to his advantage. He could hear Fischer's footsteps quickly moving away from him. The sound seemed to be coming from the tunnel on his left. Batista moved toward the entrance to that passageway. It was dark. Very dark. The only light in the entire place came from the trapdoor above. If Batista went down that tunnel, he would be doing it alone, without knowing where he was going, and in total darkness. All it would take were a few twists and turns for him to get hopelessly lost in the underground maze of confinement.

He could see the clock ticking down the seconds in his mind's eye. This was no time to let claustrophobia get the best of him. Batista took a deep breath and plunged ahead into the gloom, hoping that the sounds of footfalls that he heard weren't echoes bouncing off the walls, leading him into a dark tomb.

• • •

Chavo typed every command he could think of into the keyboard. He even risked plugging the hacking device into the computer to see if that would help.

It didn't.

When all else failed, he started banging on the escape key, over and over again.

Nothing stopped the countdown. The numbers continued to move toward zero, and toward their doom.

"Austin, I could use some help in here!" he called out. "Can you bring that guy over?"

"On my way," Austin said as he dragged the struggling security chief over to the office. Chavo looked out over the warehouse as he waited—still pressing the escape key, for lack of any other ideas. The few employees that had not fled at the first sign of trouble were mostly lying unconscious around the room. Torrie had just managed to take out the last of the workers and was following Austin as he dragged Ray over.

Once he got to the office, Ray realized that he was outnumbered, and that Fischer had abandoned him. At that point he stopped struggling. "Okay, I get it. Deal time," he said. "What say I get you into Fischer's files, and we call it even?"

"We've already got the files," Chavo said. "I need you to stop the bomb."

"What bomb?" Ray asked.

"The failsafe."

"Man, I don't know what the hell you're talking about."

Chavo's heart sank. Ray sounded genuine in his confusion. And the fear that suddenly sprang into his eyes seemed very real too. It was the look of a man who had not only just been betrayed, but pretty much knew that he had also been left to die. Chavo had originally planned to ask Austin to beat the code out of Ray, but that would be of no use now that it was clear the guy didn't even know the bomb existed. They were now depending totally on Batista to return with Fischer.

Batista wasn't sure if the tunnel was getting smaller or if it was his imagination. The walls certainly didn't seem like they were physically any closer to his body, but they still felt like they were closing in on him. He tried to put it out of his mind as he hurried through the tunnel in the direction of the sounds in front of him. Meanwhile, he did his best to keep his own footfalls as silent as he could. He had spent a lot of time on tracking detail in his NSA training. It wouldn't help if Fischer knew he was being followed. He'd just start moving faster, and since he knew where he was going, that wouldn't be a good thing. Batista's careful steps served another purpose as well. In the darkness he didn't know what was ahead of him. He could very easily fall into a hole or trip over a loose piece of concrete if he didn't pay attention. He didn't need to crack his skull and get disoriented on top of everything else.

He was getting closer to the sound of the footsteps. After a mercifully direct run, Batista turned his first corner and saw a light moving up in the distance. At that point he gave up all attempts at stealth in exchange for swiftness. Barreling forward, Batista caught up with Fischer in seconds, throwing himself on the man and taking him to the ground. Though he was no match for Batista's size, Fischer still struggled as Batista literally dragged him back to the warehouse. Thankfully, Chavo had sent Austin to the trapdoor to wait for them and help get Fischer back up into the building.

"Punch in the termination code," Chavo insisted as Austin threw Fischer back into his chair.

"There is no termination code," Fischer said. "Once the clock is started, it can't be stopped. We have to get out of here. Now."

Chavo leaned in and got close to Fischer's face. "Now, why don't I believe you?"

"Believe me or not, it won't stop the countdown," Fischer said. He leaned back in his chair trying to look calm, but Chavo could see the intense fear in his eyes. Playing the hunch, Chavo pulled over the nearest chair and sat as well. "Well, then, I guess we'll die together."

"Man, I don't need to die," Ray said from the doorway where he stood beside Stone Cold. "Fischer, give him the damn code."

"There is no code," Fischer said. "Now we should get out of here before the place blows."

Chavo looked at the screen. "It's already too late," he said. "Even if we managed to back the car out of the wreckage, we'd never clear the blast area before the toxic cloud got to us. We're already dead."

This got to Fischer. He didn't start typing out commands, but he was not leaning back in his seat any longer. The two men still had their eyes locked on each other. Growing up alongside his uncle Eddie, Chavo had played this game many times before. Though he had only been a few years older than Chavo, Eddie was a master at staring down his opponent. Throughout their youth and into adulthood Eddie had always won out, forcing Chavo to blink first. Forcing him to shy away. But not this time. Lives depended on this stare-down. And Chavo could feel his late uncle Eddie giving him extra strength from above.

As the clock counted down to under a minute,

Fischer finally broke. Chavo nearly fell back against the wall when Fischer suddenly pounced on the keyboard and typed some unknown command. The countdown immediately stopped and reset itself.

"Thanks," Chavo said, then punched Fischer in the face, knocking him out cold.

"We need to get to the dockyard," Torrie said once the excitement had finally calmed down.

"Hey, where did Ray go?" Chavo asked. Everyone had apparently been so focused on the stare-down that they had let their guards down, and Ray had taken the opportunity to slip away. Chavo would have cared more about it, but they really didn't have time. All they could do was tie up Fischer and leave him and Masterson behind for the NSA when they showed up. He was more concerned by what Torrie was filling them in on about Hunter and Cena at the Port of Newark. It seemed to him that stopping the weapons shipment was more important than some security chief at the moment. Just because Masterson was out of the picture didn't mean that one of his guys wasn't ready to fill the newly vacant position.

chapter
twenty-six

John Cena saw Hunter checking his watch once again. It had been almost an hour since they spoke with Vince. Hunter had confirmed the time at least once every five minutes since. As far as Cena could tell, it looked as if Masterson's men were hooking up the last container to the crane. Once it was loaded onto the train and secured, there would be nothing to keep those guys hanging around. With the sun rising higher, he and Hunter had already lost the cover of darkness. They were reaching now-or-never time.

"So what's the plan?" Cena asked.

"We got one of two choices," Hunter said. "We hitch a ride and track the shipment."

"And risk getting caught and killed somewhere between here and wherever the hell they're going," Cena added.

"Or we put a stop to this right now," Hunter concluded.

Cena knew what he was voting for. "Like I said, what's the plan?"

"Divide and conquer," Hunter said.

"You take that dozen guys, and I'll take the other dozen guys?"

Hunter nodded. "You take the front of the train, I'll take the back. And leave Trent to me. That guy is mine."

Cena was fine with that plan. Keep it simple, he agreed. And he was also good with the idea of letting Hunter take care of that Trent guy. Cena knew firsthand how Triple H reacted when he felt betrayed. But that was in the ring, not in life. And Cena could imagine that the revenge Hunter exacted in the ring was nothing compared to the rage he experienced in the outside world.

"And watch out for Salt and Pepper," Cena said, regarding the muscle he had the run-in with in Masterson's restaurant. There was a chance that once he and Hunter started busting heads, some of the guys out there might turn tail and run. But not Masterson's main boys. They were going to be in it to the bitter end. Best to take them out first.

Cena prepped himself for the run. He and Hunter were back in the surveillance position they had taken up at the start of this whole mess. He figured they could use the same distraction, the loading of the last container to move. Wordlessly, Hunter came to the same decision; as soon as the container was lowered into place, they looked at each other, gave a pair of double-fisted thumbs-ups, and bolted for the train.

All we have to do is stall until the cavalry arrives, Cena thought as he slipped between the train cars. Trouble was, he didn't know when that would be. Or if it was even coming.

Considering most of the action was going on toward the back of the train right now, Cena figured Triple H got the raw end of the deal. But that just meant Cena had to finish up quickly and go help the guy. He kind of liked the idea of coming to the rescue. That would burn Triple H for a good long time.

Turned out Cena had something else to deal with first. As if someone had been listening to him earlier, Masterson's two muscle-heads from the other night were heading his way. They couldn't see him between the cars at the moment, but that wouldn't last forever. Cena scrambled up the train-car ladder and took up a position on the roof to watch. There was no doubt that he could handle both these guys together in hand-to-hand combat, but the shiny metal guns sticking out of their belts evened the odds a bit. For the moment, all he could do was listen in and plot his next move.

"I haven't been able to raise Masterson on his phone," the white guy with the unfortunate face said. "That's not like him."

"Aw, he's probably just getting some from that bitch," the black guy said. Cena clenched his fists in anticipation. Even though he knew Torrie could take care of herself, he didn't like anybody talking about her that way. It had almost killed him the other night to call her that.

"Still, I don't like it," Crew Cut said. "It ain't like him."

"Well, there's nothing we can do at the moment," his buddy with the silver jewelry said. "Once we're done here, we can go check it out, a'ight."

"All right," Crew Cut said. "I'll go back and see how much longer it's gonna be."

"Yeah, Sam, you go do that," Pepper said. "Maybe if you look over their shoulders they'll move faster, you damn mother hen."

"Aw, shut the fuck up, Kel," Crew Cut said with a laugh.

Cena watched as Crew Cut slipped between the cars and hopped over to the other side where all the action was taking place, leaving his partner, Kel, all alone on the far side of the train. It was just the moment Cena had been waiting for. He peered over the edge of the train to get his bearings. Kel still had his gun, but since it was safely tucked in his pants, Cena could try to disarm the guy before he knew what hit him. Then again, between all the chains, rings, and assorted piercings the guy had on him, Cena wasn't sure if he should attack him or just throw a bucket of water on him and see if he rusted.

Cena continued to watch as the guy lit a cigarette. He wanted to give the thug a moment to relax and let his guard down. He also wanted to give the guy's buddy time to get to the other side of the train. If this one, Kel, called out, Crew Cut would be back in seconds. Conveniently, Cena could watch both sides of the train from the rooftop. "You can't see me," he whispered to himself as he tracked his prey stealthily.

Once Cena confirmed that the coast was clear on the other side, he slipped his legs over the edge and dropped himself down, keeping hold of the train for support. Once his legs were safely behind the guy's back, Cena grabbed Kel's neck in a leg lock.

Kel immediately dropped his cigarette and reached for his gun. Cena stopped the guy by twisting his legs and slamming Kel into the train car. The gun dropped from his grasp. Kel tried to yell out, but Cena had cut off his air supply. When that failed, Kel reached up and pulled on Cena's legs. The wrestler held tight, but he was at a disadvantage since Kel could pull with his entire weight. Within seconds, Cena's hands slipped off the train car, and he dropped on top of the silver-plated thug.

Both men reacted quickly, jumping to their feet with the gun halfway between the two of them.

"Go ahead," Cena said. "Try it."

There was a flash of confusion on Kel's face when he saw his attacker. Cena smiled when he realized the thug had made the connection to the other night. "Didn't expect to see me again, did you? Oh, and you can stop worrying about your friend Masterson. My girl's probably taken good care of him by now."

With a howl of anger, Kel went for the gun. Cena reacted by kicking the guy in the face and knocking him cold. Cena was almost disappointed that Kel hadn't put up more of a fight. The disappointment was short-lived when he heard a commotion off in the distance and saw that Hunter was triple-teamed by some random bad guys down on the other end of the train. Cena picked up Kel's gun and was about to run for Hunter when he heard tires screeching and saw a battered town car heading their way.

Stone Cold Steve Austin aimed the vehicle at Hunter and his little friends. He'd have to time this just right to make sure he didn't bang up Hunter in the process. Not that Austin would have minded all that much if that happened accidentally, but it would have been hell trying to explain it to Vince.

Just as he had suspected, the screeching tires had alerted the rest of the workers to their arrival. Guys were scrambling from the other side of the train, coming through the breaks between the cars like cockroaches scrambling from the light. When they saw their brethren attacking some guy, a few went to join in. Others noticed John Cena running from the far end of the train, and went after him. Still more were frozen, waiting to see where the town car ended up.

"Can I get a 'Hell, yeah'?" Austin yelled as they neared the train.

"Hell, yeah!" echoed the voices in the car.

"Hold on!" Austin slammed on the brakes and spun the wheel, swinging the car to the side and taking a trio of guys out in the process. Before the car even stopped spinning, Chavo and Batista were jumping out of the back seat, and Torrie was sliding out of the front.

"Now don't you guys go starting this street fight without me," Austin said as he swung open his door and slammed it into the back of a thug who had Hunter in a choke hold.

• • •

Chavo and Batista counted six guys running toward them, which was more than a fair fight as far as they were concerned. Batista held out his hand, and Chavo tagged himself in as the guys approached. Wordlessly, the two Superstars moved as one, mowing down the line of baddies.

A couple of the guys refused to go down so easily, which was just fine with Chavo. He took on a puny little guy who was way out of his weight class, but slippery just the same. Chavo tried several times to get a hold of the guy, but he kept slithering out of the Superstar's grasp. Finally, Chavo dropped to the ground and swept his leg out, taking the guy down. Chavo was on the little dude in a second, making sure he wasn't getting back up any time soon.

Meanwhile, Batista towered above them with his own pair of problems. Two guys not nearly as quick as their friend, but considerably larger, were taking turns keeping Batista busy. Every time Batista got a hold of one, the other would attack. They were like two giant bees buzzing around his head. But Batista knew how to deal with bees. They just needed a good swatting.

Batista lashed out both hands and grabbed both guys by their collars. In one fluid motion, he slammed the two men together. Their heads connected, and they were knocked unconscious.

At the same time Chavo had managed to put his little guy in a chokehold and knock him out. With their half-dozen fighters taken care of, they joined Hunter and Austin to deal with the rest of their enemies.

Torrie had quickly took down some loser with a well-placed kick to the groin when she saw an old friend coming her way. The thug with the crew cut was running at her, reaching for his gun and looking like he was more than happy to pay her back for what she had put him through earlier. Reacting purely by instinct, she kicked off her right heel at him, sending the shoe directly at the gun and knocking it out of his hand.

"You bitch!" he screamed as he lunged for her.

Torrie slid to the side, catching him in the gut with her fist as he missed her and blew past. "Hey, don't blame me 'cause you got beaten up by a girl," she taunted. "Oh, wait. That's right. You *can* blame me. 'Cause I was the girl."

The thug came at her again, apparently deciding to take a page from the girl fight handbook and going for her hair. This was not much of a problem, since the wig slipped right off her head when he yanked on it. Torrie could barely hold back the laughter as he tripped past her again and she sent a hard elbow to the back of the guy's head. He dropped to the ground and wasn't so quick to get back up.

"What the hell are *you* doing here?" Hunter asked Stone Cold as they fought off their attackers side by side.

"Saving your ass," Austin replied with a shit-eating grin.

Hunter just shook his head as he took out the last of his attackers with a fist to the guy's nose. There wasn't even time to watch the guy drop to the ground—Hunter had another mission in mind. In all the commotion and all the fighting, he noticed that one person was missing.

Trent!

Hunter ran between a couple cars and hopped over to the other side, where he found the missing snitch starting up a Porsche. If Hunter had seen Trent tooling around in that ride before, he would have definitely known something was up. Hunter ran over to the car as the engine revved and grabbed the doorframe. "Where do you think you're going?" he asked.

"Away from here," Trent said as he slammed on the gas and sent Hunter tumbling to the ground.

Hunter quickly hopped back up, looking for a vehicle to hotwire. There was no way in hell that he was going to let Trent get away with playing him like that. But it didn't look like Trent was getting away that easily; his car had been pointed at the train, and there was no way out that way. Hunter watched as the Porsche spun around and headed back toward him.

With only seconds until the car reached him, Hunter had a decision to make. He stood tall in the center of the road, blocking the Porsche's path. He knew that playing chicken with a car was ridiculous, but he had no other options at the moment. Hunter just stared Trent down as the Porsche approached, daring the guy to mow him down. Apparently Trent had no problem taking that dare, and he continued straight at the Superstar, forcing Hunter to dive out of the way at the last second.

Hunter heard tires screeching once again as he rolled up next to a tool shed. Trent had apparently enjoyed their game, because instead of escaping he was turning his car around for a second pass at Hunter.

As soon as he completed the turn, Trent revved the engine in a piss-poor attempt to scare Hunter. But all that did was energize the Superstar, who was looking around for something to help him take on the Porsche. He couldn't believe his luck when he saw the pile of tools stacked beside the shed. It was almost as if someone had known he was going to be there, because sitting at the top of the pile was exactly what he was looking for.

A sledgehammer.

Hunter picked up the sledgehammer and walked back out onto the road. He held out his left hand and motioned for Trent to bring it. And the asshole did just that. With tires peeling, Trent aimed the Porsche directly at Hunter. But this time, The Game was done playing. He lifted the sledgehammer, reared back, and threw it directly at the Porsche's windshield, smashing the shatterproof glass. This time, the Porsche swerved off the road, slamming into one of the metal containers.

Hunter rushed over to the car and nearly yanked the driver's-side door right off its hinges. Inside, a bleary-eyed and bloody Trent was doing his best to stay conscious. "Like I said before . . . where *the hell* do you think you're going?" Hunter punctuated his question with a fist to Trent's face, knocking the guy out cold. He then joined the rest of the Superstars for mopping up.

Once all the criminals were tied up, all the Superstars could do was wait for the NSA guys to take them in. It was almost an hour before Thompson returned from the warehouse, since it had taken a while for Vince to break through the communications blackout. That had only happened once Thompson turned his phone back on after finding Fischer and Masterson tied to a barrel of toxic waste in the warehouse.

The NSA director gave the WWE Superstars a

simple "Good job" before starting the operation of processing the criminals. That was okay, though. They had neither wanted nor expected anything more. This was exactly the kind of thing they had signed on for. They were just doing their jobs.

And speaking of jobs, it was Torrie that reminded them of the fact that they only had twenty minutes to get to Madison Square Garden for that press event Vince had told them they weren't supposed to miss.

"Do you think we can borrow some cars from these NSA guys?" Torrie asked.

Triple H looked at the train in front of them. It would only take a minute to disconnect the engine from the cars. And the Garden *was* built on top of Penn Station. "Well," he said with a grin, "we do have a train."

Epilogue

The Garden crowd had been hot all night. This episode of *Raw* was already going down in the history books as one of the best, and the fans were eating it up. Like any other audience, they had already come in looking for a good time, and their cheers continued to build and shake the building as every minute passed. Since the opening bell, these fans had watched their favorite WWE Superstars compete in the matches of their lives. There were stunning upsets, humorous hijinks, and moves that, quite frankly, probably weren't all that legal.

Then, just as the main event—Triple H vs. John Cena—was ending with a crowd-disappointing double DQ, Vince McMahon made a surprise appearance. Triple H and Cena were incredulous as he stepped into the ring right in the middle of the action. Vince looked out into the crowd and basked in their warm cheers, ignoring the fact that those cheers were actually boos and chants of "Asshole!" He ignored Triple H and Cena too. He had more important things in mind.

Vince flipped on his microphone and made the stunning announcement. There was still one more match to go. He was calling out every Superstar, man and woman, who competed this evening to compete in a battle royal with Stone Cold Steve Austin as special guest referee.

The crowd freaked out. It was pandemonium as the Superstars started filing out from backstage, looking both confused and ready to go. At that moment, Vince had the fans in the palm of his hand, but he knew he'd lose them if he stayed a moment longer. This wasn't his show. This was for his Superstars. As the wrestlers prepared, he dashed into the back, wanting to get to the safety of his office so he could watch the proceedings from there.

The match had already begun by the time he

opened the door to his private backstage office. But he wasn't able to enjoy it because he had a surprise visitor waiting behind his desk. Out of habit, the first thing that came to Vince's mind was, *What's next?*

"Even in school I knew you could stir up a crowd, but this is unreal," Phil Thompson said.

"You're in my chair," Vince replied.

Thompson smiled, but he also got up. "Touchy, touchy."

Vince turned his chair so that he could watch the match. The added benefit was that he got to turn his back on Thompson to do it. The two men remained in silence for a few minutes as they watched Rob Van Dam and Big Show get taken down.

"You had no right to assign Austin a mission without informing me," Vince finally said.

"They're called *secret* agents for a reason, Vince," Thompson replied. "I figured you of all people would get that."

"I don't like to be played," Vince said. "You led me to believe that my Superstars were superfluous. Like they weren't good enough for the real work."

"Did you really think their training was over just because they left the NSA facility? It takes years to become an operative. You should have more faith in me."

"Right," Vince said. "Considering our past history, you're surprised there are trust issues."

"Okay, I deserved that," Thompson ceded. "And you're right. I didn't think most of your Superstars were ready for the big boys like Masterson. I figured it would be best to give them time to see how they performed. Well, you proved me wrong. They don't need to wait. They know what they're doing, alone *and* as a team."

"Glad you can see the obvious," Vince said.

"Glad you can make this easy for me," Thompson replied, heavy with sarcasm. When Vince said nothing more, Thompson dropped a file on the chairman's desk.

"What's that?" Vince asked.

"A preliminary report on this human-trafficking ring crossing from Mexico into Texas," Thompson said. "Read it. Let me know what you think. And you may want to share it with some of your Superstars too."

Vince let out a rare smile as Thompson left the office, then flipped through the file, looking over the photos and information. It looked like it was going to be big. Certainly something he'd need a few guys working on. When he hit the last page, he opened the desk drawer and dropped the file inside. There would be time for that later. He had more important things to do at the moment. He turned his attention back to the monitor.

The crowd inside the Garden had just let out a roar that he heard through the walls. Inside the ring, Edge had just been eliminated from the match, and they were down to a final four Superstars: Batista, Chavo Guerrero, John Cena, and Triple H.

There they were. His team. Sure, there were other Superstars involved in the NSA's work, but these were the ones that had proven their mettle this week. The ones that were responsible for upping their profile. They were a force to be reckoned with. Sure, in the ring they might be hampered by old rivalries and shifting alliances, but outside, in the real world, they would continue to work together to take down whatever was thrown at them. They were not only wrestling Superstars—they were American heroes.

Vince watched as the remaining wrestlers paused to bask in the moment. It was almost as though Vince could read their thoughts as they all looked at each other. He could see the respect in their eyes, and the camaraderie.

But he could also see the fight that they all still had left in them.

The moment was over.

John Cena blindsided Batista, while Chavo charged Triple H.

As many as 1 in 3 Americans
have HIV and don't know it.

TAKE CONTROL.
KNOW YOUR STATUS.
GET TESTED.

To learn more about HIV testing,
or get a free guide to HIV and
other sexually transmitted diseases.

www.knowhivaids.org
1-866-344-KNOW

09620

Not sure what to read next?

Visit Pocket Books online at
www.simonsays.com

Reading suggestions for
you and your reading group
New release news
Author appearances
Online chats with your favorite writers
Special offers
Order books online
And much, much more!

POCKET BOOKS
A Division of Simon & Schuster
A VIACOM COMPANY

POCKET
STAR BOOKS
A Division of Simon & Schuster
A VIACOM COMPANY

13456